THE BLUEBIRD
AND
THE SPARROW

Books by Janette Oke

Another Homecoming*
Tomorrow's Dream*

CANADIAN WEST

When Calls the Heart   When Breaks the Dawn
When Comes the Spring   When Hope Springs New

Beyond the Gathering Storm
When Tomorrow Comes

LOVE COMES SOFTLY

Love Comes Softly   Love's Unending Legacy
Love's Enduring Promise   Love's Unfolding Dream
Love's Long Journey   Love Takes Wing
Love's Abiding Joy   Love Finds a Home

A PRAIRIE LEGACY

The Tender Years   A Quiet Strength
A Searching Heart   Like Gold Refined

SEASONS OF THE HEART

Once Upon a Summer   Winter Is Not Forever
The Winds of Autumn   Spring's Gentle Promise

SONG OF ACADIA*

The Meeting Place   The Birthright
The Sacred Shore   The Distant Beacon
The Beloved Land

WOMEN OF THE WEST

The Calling of Emily Evans   A Bride for Donnigan
Julia's Last Hope   Heart of the Wilderness
Roses for Mama   Too Long a Stranger
A Woman Named Damaris   The Bluebird and the Sparrow
They Called Her Mrs. Doc   A Gown of Spanish Lace
The Measure of a Heart   Drums of Change

———

Janette Oke: A Heart for the Prairie
Biography of Janette Oke by Laurel Oke Logan

*with T. Davis Bunn

JANETTE OKE

THE BLUEBIRD
AND
THE SPARROW

BETHANYHOUSE

MINNEAPOLIS, MINNESOTA

The Bluebird and the Sparrow
Copyright © 1995
Janette Oke

Cover design by Lookout Design, Inc.

Published by Bethany House Publishers
11400 Hampshire Avenue South
Bloomington, Minnesota 55438

Bethany House Publishers is a division of
Baker Publishing Group, Grand Rapids, Michigan.

Printed in the United States of America

ISBN-13: 978-0-7642-0253-7
ISBN-10: 0-7642-0253-7

The Library of Congress has cataloged the original edition as follows:

Oke, Janette, 1935-
    The bluebird and the sparrow / Janette Oke.
        p.   cm. — (Women of the West)

    I. Title.   II. Series: Oke, Janette 1935-   Women of the West.
PR9199.3.O38B57   1994
813'.54—dc20   94-49703
ISBN 1-55661-612-0 Trade Paper   CIP
ISBN 1-55661-613-9 Large Print

JANETTE OKE was born in Champion, Alberta, to a Canadian prairie farmer and his wife, and she grew up in a large family full of laughter and love. She is a graduate of Mountain View Bible College in Alberta, where she met her husband, Edward, and they were married in May of 1957. After pastoring churches in Indiana and Canada, the Okes spent some years in Calgary, where Edward served in several positions on college faculties while Janette continued her writing. She has written over four dozen novels for adults and children, and her book sales now approach thirty million copies.

The Okes have three sons and one daughter, all married, and are enjoying their dozen grandchildren. Edward and Janette are active in their local church and make their home near Didsbury, Alberta.

Contents

Chapter One

The Gift

In spite of an eerie stillness about the house, people seemed in an awful hurry whenever they passed from one room to another. *Bustling—that's what Mama calls it*, observed three-year-old Berta, curled up in an overstuffed chair, waiting.

Waiting.

It seemed to her that she had been waiting forever. Why was it—whatever *it* was—taking so long?

She sighed a deep sigh, pushed back dark hair that wanted to hang in her eyes, and rearranged her sitting position.

If only—*if only* someone would stop and tell her what was happening.

She heard quick steps in the hall again and another scurrying person entered the room. It was Mrs. Pringle, a neighbor. Berta uncurled her legs and jumped to the rug.

"Where's Mama?" Berta asked before the woman could hurry on by.

Mrs. Pringle seemed to slide to a stop. She looked at the young child and her eyes softened.

"She's—she's in her room. She—"

"Doesn't she got the baby yet?" asked Berta impatiently.

"No. No—not yet. Soon. The doctor says soon—now." The answer was not what Berta wished to hear.

"Why does it take so long?" she asked, her voice filled with annoyance. "I wanna see Mama."

"Now, you just try to be patient," soothed the neighbor woman. "Your mother is—is quite busy at the moment."

She turned purposefully away to fulfil whatever mission she had set out to do.

Berta turned, too—back to her overstuffed chair. She crawled up on it and tucked her feet back under herself. If Mama saw her, she'd scold. But Mama couldn't see her. Not from the bedroom where she had gone to get the new baby—ages and ages ago. Berta took a bit of satisfaction from the fact that she was alone and able to put her feet up if she wished to. Yet guilt made her spread her skirts carefully over the tips of her shoes so they would be hidden from sight.

I don't know why it takes so long, she stormed again to herself. *Mama's been gone all day. All day. And Papa— Papa—*

Berta had never been deserted in such a complete fashion in all her three years. She hated to be alone. She didn't like the hushed suspense that hung around her. She didn't like the hurrying of people who didn't even stop to talk to her. And she didn't think she was going to care much for that new baby, either. Already her cozy world had been changed.

Berta curled up against the back of the chair, stuffed fists against her eyes, and began to cry.

———

Even after the word finally came that she had a little sister, Berta was unable to see her mother.

"Not tonight," her father told her as he cuddled her close on his lap and shared the good news.

"You have a baby sister. She's strong and healthy— and—and beautiful." And Berta had seen tears in her father's eyes. It was the first time she had ever seen her father close to weeping. It disturbed her. She squirmed and turned her back on the uncomfortable sight. Was the new baby making her father cry too?

"And Mama is fine. Just fine," her father went on, his voice breaking.

Berta turned to stare into his face. If Mama was fine, what was making her papa's eyes water and his voice sound funny?

"Why can't I see her?" asked Berta.

"Mama is very tired tonight. She—"

"Why?" Berta was persistent. She stared into her father's ashen face.

"Getting a new baby is very hard work," her father informed her quietly. "And Mama had some—some difficulty—"

"Then why didn't she just leave it," said Berta emphatically, her hands punctuating her words. She missed her mother.

Her father's lips twisted with a hint of a smile. He pulled Berta back against his chest and brushed her hair away from her face.

"You wait until you see your new sister," he said, and his mood seemed to lighten. "She's a beautiful little girl. You'll have so much fun. She'll be a wonderful playmate."

"But I wanna see Mama."

"In the morning. First thing in the morning I will take you to see Mama."

"Why can't I see her now?"

"Because. Because she's very tired. The doctor has given her some medicine to help her sleep. She needs to rest."

"But I—"

"Don't make trouble, Berta."

Her father's voice sounded—different, strained.

"Are you sick?" she asked quickly.

"No. No—just very, very tired," he answered. "I think we all need a good sleep." He glanced up at the wall calendar and seemed to muse aloud. "June sixth, eighteen ninety-four—the longest day of my life. It's truly been a long ordeal."

Berta had no idea what an ordeal was—but she understood that it was not a pleasant circumstance, and she linked it to the new baby.

———

Berta was taken to her mother's room the next morning as promised. Her father took her by the hand and led her there. It did not feel quite right to be tippy-toeing through the house as though someone was sick or sleeping. She had so hoped that by morning things would be put back to normal.

Her mother usually was never still in bed at this time in the morning. Something about seeing her lying there brought fear to the small girl's heart. She wanted to ask her father, but there was no time. They were standing beside the bed, looking at her mother, who lay pale and limp against the white bedclothes. Her eyes were closed. Her hair was scattered about her shoulders and the white pillow. Berta turned quickly to her father, her eyes large with questions. Before she could ask any of them her mother stirred.

"Berta," she murmured. "Berta," she said in just the

same way she had always spoken the name. "Come up here beside me, dear," and she patted the quilt with her hand.

Berta felt herself being lifted up and placed beside her mother on the bed. Then her mother's arm was about her—patting her shoulder, giving her a hug.

"Have you seen your new sister?" asked her mama.

Berta shook her head. "I wanted to see you," she said, her lips trembling.

The arm about her tightened. "I've missed you," her mother said in a whispery voice.

"I missed you, too," said Berta. "It took a long time—"

"Yes. Yes—it did take a long time. But it was worth it. Every minute of it. You'll think so too. Just wait—wait until you see your new baby sister. She's beautiful."

Her mother smiled.

Berta squirmed, still uncomfortable about the new baby. She changed the subject. "It's time to get up," she announced to her mother. "We're gonna have breakfast now."

Berta couldn't understand why her mother and father both chuckled.

"Mama won't be getting up for breakfast today," her father said. "She'll have her breakfast in bed."

"Why?" asked Berta.

"Mama needs to stay in bed and rest for several days," her father explained. "It's hard work getting a new baby sister. Mama needs lots of rest."

Berta felt confused. Then angry. If it was such hard work—if it rearranged all of life—if it kept her mother from her—then why bother with a new baby?

She slipped from her mother's arm and slid down the side of the bed. "I want breakfast," she said without looking at her mother or her father, and she started for the door.

"Don't you want to see your new sister?" called her mother after her.

Berta shook her head and kept right on walking. "I want breakfast," she repeated. "I'm hungry."

Her father followed her from the room.

There were many visits to her mother's room. And Berta was introduced to the new baby sister. At first she found it hard to believe her eyes. This new baby was scarcely big enough to be seen on Mama's arm. She was all bundled in blankets, the only thing showing being a tiny little face with an open mouth. Her mama would laugh and say that she was hungry, but it seemed to Berta that she was always hungry.

Berta was prompted to hold the baby on her own lap, with support from Mrs. Pringle, who was staying to care for the family. Mama smiled her pleasure and Mrs. Pringle clucked, and Berta looked down at the little bundle of blankets.

The baby's head was moving, her open mouth twisting this way and that. Berta feared for a moment that the small infant might turn and bite her. Then the small, squinty eyes opened. It was the first that Berta had seen the baby with open eyes. It seemed that the new baby sister looked right into her face.

"Oh, look," cried her mother joyfully. "She is looking at you. She wants to see who her big sister is."

Mrs. Pringle joined in the little celebration. "Look at that. Just look at that," she exclaimed. "She's checking ya out—an' that's fer sure."

For a moment—for one brief moment—something stirred within the heart of the little girl. The baby was looking at her. Her baby.

And then the squirming little mite turned her head and began to search with open mouth again. The little red face screwed up in protest and the noise that Berta already had learned to hate came again. The spell was broken. Berta pulled back from the baby and began to push her off her lap. Mrs. Pringle's hands took over.

"She's hungry," the woman said as though an explanation was needed. And she took the baby, clucking and cooing as she went, over to her mother.

Berta scooted down from the chair and headed for the door. She was leaving. If there was no one in the kitchen she'd get herself a cookie from the cookie jar.

Mother was finally up and about the house once again. Mrs. Pringle went back to her home. Berta was prepared to welcome life back to normal again.

Only things didn't go back to the way they had been. There was the new baby—and it seemed that the new baby needed an unbelievable amount of her mother's time. There were bath times and feeding times and changing times and fussy times—and Berta found herself continually on her own. She didn't like it. She missed her mother.

Oh, there still were times when she could help her mother in the kitchen. Still story times while little Glenna slept. Still snuggling on her father's lap or shared visits to the woods or meadows. Still prayers at bedtime and hugs throughout the day—but it wasn't the same.

Berta wished they would just send the baby back.

"Mama, look. She's got my finger."

Mrs. Berdette looked up from the sock she was darning and smiled at her two daughters.

"I think she likes her big sister," she said softly.

Berta's eyes shone as she looked at her baby sister. Glenna had grown already. But it was hard for Berta to remember how little she had once been. She still seemed so small. So helpless.

"Remember I told you that she would be a playmate almost before you know it?" asked Mrs. Berdette.

Berta nodded.

"Well . . . she's already wanting to play."

"I'll get my tea set," offered Berta generously.

"Oh no," her mother quickly explained. "She's not big enough for that yet."

"What can she do?" asked Berta, her spirits dampened.

"Well . . . so far she can just smile . . . and hold fingers. But soon she will be able to hold small things—toys . . . her toes. She'll keep on growing—and changing. And one day—before you know it—she will be able to sit up and play."

It seemed to Berta that it was taking an awfully long time to get the playmate she had been promised. She pulled her finger out of the baby's grip and went to pick out one of her books.

"Will you read to me?" she asked her mother.

"I'll read after Glenna is down for her nap. She's going to want to nurse soon. We wouldn't have time to finish the story."

Her mother laid aside the sock and yarn and reached up to massage tired neck muscles. She still looked weary.

Berta sat down on the floor rug with her book spread out in her lap. She'd picture-read the book to herself.

Chapter Two

Growth

"She's lovely! Look at those curls. Those blue eyes. She's just beautiful!"

Berta was used to the words. Whenever ladies came to the house or met her mother on the streets there were the same remarks. Everyone was always exclaiming over Glenna.

Berta shut out the voices and turned another page in her new picture book. Two small children played with a puppy dog on a wide green lawn. Berta wished she had a puppy. If she asked her mother, would a dog be allowed? She already had asked her father. He had made some little speech about it being bad timing. A puppy and a baby didn't mix well, he had said with a smile. Berta cast a quick glance in the direction of small Glenna and the cooing women. Maybe one of the ladies could be persuaded to take Glenna home with her.

Then Berta let her gaze go to her mother. No. Mama would never allow it. She seemed totally taken with the new one. Her face glowed, her eyes shone. She was nodding in total agreement to all that the visitor was saying. Glenna was beautiful.

Berta returned to her book. She flipped another page, angry that the two book-children could have a puppy when all she had was a sister.

Molly, her mama's part-time help, brought in a tea tray and cookies. Berta laid her book aside and joined the ladies still fussing over the baby. Glenna was smiling and cooing and blowing small baby bubbles as two visitors and her mama coaxed and chortled and oohed and aahed. Berta decided that she didn't want cookies after all. She picked up her picture book and headed for the door.

"Berta," her mother surprised her by calling. "Aren't you going to have tea with us?"

Berta shook her head. Her bobbed straight hair bounced around her face, slapping her gently on each cheek. She liked the feel of her hair. She shook her head more vigorously.

"We're having your favorite cookies," encouraged her mother.

Berta was torn. She loved the sugar cookies with the almond slices scattered over the tops.

"Molly has brought your glass of milk," coaxed her mother.

Still Berta hesitated.

Mrs. Berdette turned to her guests. "Berta is my big helper," she informed the ladies. "I don't know how I'd manage without her. She runs little errands for me all day long. And baby Glenna just loves her big sister. She smiles more—"

Suddenly Berta's mind was made up. She had been about to stay, but when the attention turned once again to the baby, she decided against it.

She dropped her head so that her hair fell forward, gently brushing at her cheeks.

"Come," invited her mother, patting the footstool by her chair.

Berta shook her head. Something within her rebelled. Without being able to put it into words, she knew instinctively that her leaving would make her mother feel sad, and that gave her a strange bit of power. That something within made her want to use that power to hurt her mother just a little bit. Not a big hurt. Just enough to make her mother sorry that she had fussed over Glenna with the visiting ladies.

Berta's chin came up defiantly, her dark eyes darkening even further with resolve. "I don't want cookies," she said firmly. "I want to go swing."

Her mother did look sad. Berta felt a moment of pleasure. Then her mother's face brightened and she smiled. "Very well," she said gently. "You may go swing if you wish."

A little of the victory was gone from the moment when her mother gave approval. And her mother was smiling again. Berta wasn't sure if she had won or lost. She tossed her new book on the chair by the door and fled the room to the back veranda.

It was hard to dislike Glenna. From her very first awareness, she seemed to adore her big sister. Even Berta could sense it. From the moment the baby glimpsed her in the morning until the time she was tucked in at night, she favored Berta with her squeals and giggles and full attention.

At those rare times when the two little ones were left in a room on their own, Berta could not resist her baby sister. But she didn't want her mother to notice.

Without knowing the word, Berta understood that they were in competition, her baby sister and her. Competition for her mother's time and attention. Berta tried

every trick she knew in order to defeat her little oppo-
nent—but all Glenna had to do was screw up her pretty
little face and cry, and Mama dropped whatever they
were doing together and went for the infant. Berta had
even tried the crying trick herself—but found it didn't
work nearly as well for her. Mama had soothed, comforted—but from a distance. Her arms were already
filled with baby Glenna.

"Just a minute," her mama would say. "As soon as
Glenna is finished nursing I'll rock you and we'll read a
story."

But Berta didn't want to wait for Glenna. It meant
that Glenna had won again. She decided then and there
that she would not use the crying trick again. Glenna
would always be the winner in that game.

So Berta subconsciously looked for new methods to
contend with this tiny interloper. She wasn't sure what
they should be. But she wouldn't borrow Glenna's ways.
That much she knew. Berta gradually came to the conclusion that whatever Glenna was, she would not be.
Whatever Glenna did, she would not do. Whatever
Glenna liked, she would not like. She would be the op-
posite of her baby sister. They would see, with time,
which one would be the victor.

———

"How many more sleeps?" asked the small Glenna.

Mrs. Berdette brushed back the silky curls and
smiled at her three-year-old daughter. "This is the last
sleep," she informed her.

"Chris'as is next?"

"Next," agreed her mother.

Glenna scampered down from her mother's knee and
rushed over to Berta. "Berty," she exclaimed, eyes shin-

ing with delight, "Chris'as is next."

"Not 'next,' " Berta said with six-year-old superiority. "In the morning, Glenna. Christmas—" she pronounced the word with emphasized correctness, "Christmas is in the morning."

Glenna nodded, her curls bouncing with each nod. "Uh huh—next day mornin'," she agreed.

Berta lifted her head and sighed and cast a glance of exasperation toward her father.

"She never gets it right," said Berta.

Her father chuckled. "Well, if you want to be up bright and early to see what your stockings will hold—I think it's time to tuck in," he said and rose from his chair.

Berta cast a glimpse at the fireplace, where two small stockings hung on the mantel.

"But I—" she began.

Glenna was already heading for the door, her small bare feet pattering on the polished oak floor.

"Berty—come," she called, turning and extending her hand toward her big sister. "Let's sleep. Papa said."

"You hush up, Glenna," Berta retorted sharply. "I heard Papa."

"Berta," said her father sternly. "Is that any way to talk to your little sister?"

Berta studied his face to measure his mood. "She— she always thinks she's my boss," she defended herself.

"She was just inviting you to join her for bedtime," put in her mother.

"I'm six," she insisted, "an' she's only three. I know when to go to bed."

"Then why aren't you on your way?" asked her father.

He didn't sound angry. Not yet. Berta wasn't sure if she dared to press further.

She dared.

"I will as soon as I finish this puzzle," she said, tipping her head to one side, defiance tilting her chin. She was reversing his decision.

"The puzzle will wait for morning," her father said and stood to his feet. His voice sounded firm—and commanding.

"But I'm almost—" she began.

Glenna still stood at the door, concern showing on her tiny face because of the tension in the room. Papa had said one thing. Berta was defying his order. Everyone soon would be unhappy. Glenna did not like discord. Glenna loved to have people smiling—happy.

"Berty—come," she said again.

It was more than Berta could bear. She turned from her puzzle, her hand sweeping it onto the floor with one quick movement. "You just hush, Glenna," she said, her chin quivering, her eyes blinking back tears that she refused to let fall. "I'll go when—"

She had been going to say "when I want to," but her father's voice cut the sentence short.

"Berta!" His voice was sharp.

She hated to lift her eyes. She did not wish to see the looks on the faces in the room. Her father would look so stern—so big. Her mother would look sad—maybe even be fighting tears. And Glenna—Glenna would be looking like a little frightened puppy. Berta had seen the look before. She didn't like it—that look on Glenna's face. That pleading, teary-eyed look that told Berta that the little girl both adored and wished to defend her. Berta did not want Glenna to be on her team. Nor going to her defense. Glenna—Glenna always, *always* pleaded for everyone. Berta did not want or need Glenna's championing.

"Pick up the puzzle," said her father.

Berta still did not look up.

There was a pattering of feet somewhere behind her. "I'll help," came a small voice.

"No, Glenna," spoke her father. "Berta scattered the puzzle pieces—Berta will pick them up."

Berta did not look up. She knew that she'd look into the eyes of a sympathetic Glenna. She did not wish to look at her. Nor did she wish to look into the commanding eyes of her father—or the teary eyes of her mother.

She bent her head forward before she knelt to the rug. Slowly—ever so slowly, she began to pick up the pieces of scattered puzzle. One by one she laid them in the box before her. At long last she reached for the final piece before her. The family members in the room had been holding their collective breath.

"You missed one," said her father. "Behind you."

Berta turned, retrieved the last piece, and slowly laid it in the box with the others.

"Now—it is bedtime," said her father.

Berta did not argue. Without lifting her head she stood to her feet and turned to walk toward the door. Glenna pattered up beside her and reached to take her hand.

But Berta pulled her hand away. She did not want to be escorted to her room by the small Glenna.

"We'll be in to hear your prayers," called her mother after her.

Berta did not look forward to the prayer time. She wished she could fall asleep before they had time to come. Maybe if she pretended . . .

The two small girls were in the long hall. Glenna reached for her hand again.

Berta jerked her hand away. "Don't, Glenna," she said as angrily as her whispered words could be hissed. "You—you bother me."

Glenna's eyes filled with tears. "Don't be sad, Berty," she pleaded. "It's Chris'as—next day mornin'."

The words only served to remind Berta how it had all

started. She cast an angry glance at her little sister and marched stiffly down the hall to their room.

————

When Berta opened her eyes, darkness still pressed against her window. She had completely forgotten the unpleasantness of the night before. But she had not forgotten that this was Christmas morning. For one moment she lay still and listened for sounds in the house. Was it time to be up? Had anyone else in the household stirred? Would she be sent back to bed if she crawled out and made her way toward the living room with its warm fire and the stockings over the mantel?

Very faintly she heard hushed voices. Then soft laughter. Her mother and father were already up.

Berta threw back the covers and slid to the floor. She didn't pause to put on her slippers.

"Glenna. Glenna," she called across the room. "It's time. It's Christmas."

The tiny girl stirred.

"It's Christmas," Berta said again. She was beside Glenna's bed now, one hand extended to touch her little sister's arm.

With a smile Glenna wakened. "Chris'as?" she repeated. "Now?"

"Now," answered Berta.

Together they ran down the hall and toward the light in the living room. Already Berta could feel the warmth of the fire that spilled out into the chilly hallway. Already she could smell the scent of hot, spiced apple cider, her parents' favorite Christmas morning drink. It was Christmas. Her favorite time of the year. She outran Glenna.

"Merry Christmas," called her mother as Berta burst into the room.

"Merry Christmas," echoed her father, who was busy tossing another log onto the open fire.

"Oh-h," squealed Glenna from somewhere behind her. "A dolly."

Berta lifted her eyes. Yes. Dollies. Beautiful dollies gazed out at them from two full stockings. Berta's breath caught in her throat. She slid to a stop and her hands clasped together in front of her. One doll was dressed in soft pink. The other in delicate blue. Each wore a bonnet with lacy frills and loops of ribbon. Berta still held her breath.

"Can you get, Papa?" pleaded Glenna, her arms extended toward the stocking above her reach.

With a satisfied smile her father lifted down the stocking and placed it in Glenna's arms.

"Mine too. Mine too!" cried Berta.

The second stocking was lifted down. Berta squatted on the rug before the warm fire and lifted the doll tenderly from its place. She didn't even think to explore what else the stocking held. She gazed at the pretty doll before her, fingering the soft curls, trailing her hand over the lacy frills of the blue gown. She was beautiful.

"Look," squealed Glenna. "She has bloomers!"

Berta turned to look. Glenna had the doll tipped upside down, its multi-skirts hoisted in a crumpled state while she studied the pantaloons.

"Don't, Glenna," said Berta sharply. "You are messing her."

Glenna quickly turned her doll right side up and smoothed down the skirts. "She has," she insisted, nodding her head to emphasize her point. "She has bloomers."

Berta gently smoothed her doll's soft cape. "Mine's got

a prettier dress," she murmured.

"An' she has shoes," went on Glenna without answering her sister's comment.

Berta looked at the tiny feet. Yes, there were real leather slippers. Slippers that had buttons.

Berta looked at Glenna's doll. Glenna was struggling with the buttons. Already one tiny shoe lay on the floor beside her.

"Don't, Glenna," scolded Berta. "You mustn't undress her. You'll ruin her—"

"Berta," her mother spoke softly. "It's Glenna's dolly. Let her play with it as she wishes."

"Why don't you see what else is in your stocking," prompted her father, "and then we'll have breakfast."

Both girls eagerly retrieved their stockings and began to pull out the rest of the contents. Glenna squealed over each item. Berta surveyed each new possession in silence. Though she was pleased with each gift, nothing—*nothing*—matched the beautiful doll. She carefully carried it to the breakfast table with her and reluctantly laid it aside as she ate her breakfast.

Chapter Three

A Family Outing

"We need to get you dressed so we can go to Grandmother's house," announced Mrs. Berdette as soon as the girls had finished their breakfast and gathered their dolls back into their arms.

"'Ray," cheered Glenna on behalf of both of them. They loved to go to their grandmother's.

"Will Ada be there?" asked Berta. She enjoyed playing with a cousin her own age.

"Yes—Ada and William and little Dorcas."

"And Unca Cee?" chimed in Glenna.

"Aunt Cee," corrected Berta. "It's Aunt Cee."

"Aunt Cee," repeated Glenna.

"One of these days you're going to have to learn how to say Cecily," laughed their father.

"An' Unca John?" asked Glenna, casting a glance at Berta to see if she would be corrected again.

"Uncle John," agreed her mother.

"'Ray," cheered Glenna again.

"You may wear your new dresses," her mother went on. This brought another cheer.

"An' a big ribbon in my hair?" asked Glenna.

Her mother smiled. "A great big ribbon in your hair," she answered the girl.

"I don't want a ribbon in my hair," said Berta firmly.

Glenna looked disappointed. "Ribbons look pretty," she told her older sister.

"I don't want to look pretty," maintained Berta.

"Why?" asked Glenna innocently.

"Just 'cause I don't. That's all."

Glenna looked sad. "Granna likes us lookin' pretty," she dared to say.

"Berta doesn't need to wear a ribbon if she doesn't wish to," Mrs. Berdette gently pointed out to stop the discussion.

Glenna still looked unhappy. "Granna—"

"I don't need to wear a ribbon if I don't want to, Glenna. Mama said so," said Berta, her chin lifting.

Glenna looked about to cry. Then her face brightened, and she reached out and patted her big sister's arm. "That's all right, Berta," she soothed with little-girl tenderness. "Granna will unnerstand."

Berta pulled away. She didn't need her little sister taking her side.

They dressed in the new dresses that Mama had sewed for them. It had taken her many hours at the new Singer Papa had bought for her birthday. The dresses were full and frilly and generously bedecked with ribbons. Glenna twirled so that the skirt would bounce, making herself dizzy in the process. Berta wished to twirl too, but she refused to allow herself the pleasure. Still she could not deny a stolen glance into the mirror on the wall of Mama's room. It nearly took her breath away. She looked—she looked like the princess in her new Christmas book. For one brief moment she was tempted to relent and have her mother place the loops of matching ribbon in her hair.

"Look at me," chirped Glenna. "I look like a ferny."

"Ferny? You mean fairy, Glenna. Fairy," corrected Berta.

"Fairy," repeated Glenna, spinning again. Then she stopped and turned to her mother. "Put in my bow, Mama. Put in my ribbons so I'll look just like a fairy."

Berta turned and walked away. She would not have a bow in her hair.

"I need my baby," Glenna said from behind her.

"It's not a baby, Glenna. It's a dolly," informed Berta, whirling around to look at her sister.

Glenna did not argue. "I need her," she said again.

Berta had already put her new doll up on her cupboard shelf beside her stuffed bear and dog.

"We're gonna go," Berta told her sister. "Papa's already getting the team."

"I wanna take her," said Glenna. "I wanna take her to Granna's."

"You can't take her. She'll get all mussed up," said Berta with grown-up firmness.

"I wanna," said Glenna and her eyes began to tear. "I wanna play with her."

"You can take her if you wish," Mrs. Berdette told her. "That's what she's for. To play with."

She left the room, calling back over her shoulder, "Papa will soon be here with the team. I need to get the food together."

Berta listened to her mother's footsteps retreat down the hallway. She turned to Glenna.

"If you play with her she'll get all mussed," she argued.

Glenna picked up her doll and hugged her close.

"You're already mussing her," continued Berta.

Glenna looked alarmed. She thrust her doll back and studied her carefully. "She isn't mussed, Berty," she said finally. But she laid the doll back down and smoothed at her skirts.

But Berta had already changed her mind. It would serve Glenna right if she ruined her doll. "Go ahead— take her," she said with a shrug. "Go ahead."

With a joyous look Glenna picked up her doll and clasped her close. "Thanks, Berty," she said with a smile.

Berta tossed her head, making her hair brush against her cheeks.

"I need a blankie," Glenna went on. "She'll get cold."

Berta cast a glance at her younger sister. She was so silly.

"I know," brightened Glenna. "I'll use my towel."

And Glenna hurried off to pull her towel off its hook in the bathroom. Then she bundled her baby in haphazard fashion, concealing even her pretty face.

She's really gonna mess her up, thought Berta, but she didn't say the words out loud. The thought gave her a moment of strange satisfaction.

———

Berta always enjoyed the trip to Grandmother's house—but never more so than on Christmas Day. Bundled up snugly against the sharp cold and tucked among blankets on the soft hay of the cutter, she squinted against the brightness of the morning sun and studied the frost-painted branches of the barren trees overhead.

"I think my nose is leakin'," said Glenna to no one in particular. Mrs. Berdette slipped off a glove and turned, hankie in hand, to wipe the child's nose.

"It's nippy," said Mrs. Berdette, tucking her hankie back in the pocket of her long dark coat.

"Are we there yet?" asked Glenna as she sniffed.

"We just started out," answered Berta in annoyance.

"We can't be there yet when we just started."

But even the angry words could not dampen the spirits of the small girl. She began to sing.

"Silen' night. Ho'ey night,
Allas calm. Allas bright."

Berta covered her ears. She couldn't stand to hear the song sung incorrectly, but she knew if she protested, her mother and father would take Glenna's part. They enjoyed hearing their little girl sing.

———

There was a wild and joyous welcome at Grandmother's house. Cousins ran forward with excited words about what Christmas had brought. Aunt Cee kissed everyone and Uncle John boomed out cheery greetings in his man-sized voice while Grandmother beamed and hugged and said over and over how glad she was to see them and how much they had grown since the last visit.

Already the house was filled with delicious scents, promising another of Grandmother's wonderful Christmas dinners. But after one deep sniff, Berta pushed aside thoughts of dinner. She could hardly wait for the greetings to be over so she could slip out of her coat and show off her pretty new dress.

But Glenna was helped with her coat first.

"Just look at you," exclaimed Grandmother. "Aren't you a picture?"

"Ah-h," said Aunt Cee. "What a dolly."

Glenna pushed forward her smothered doll. "In here. My dolly," she informed them all, and she began to unwind the bath towel.

Aunt Cee laughed and helped the child find the new doll in all the bundling.

Grandmother turned her attention to Berta.

"And look at you," she said, her eyes shining. "My, how you've grown. And you have a pretty dress, too. How nice you look. And so grown-up."

After all the attention Glenna had just received, Berta was anxious to forget the new dress. "I can read," she informed her grandmother proudly, thrusting forth the book she had brought.

"Read? Already? You must read for me—after dinner."

Berta was disappointed that she'd have to wait. She wanted to steal the attention back from Glenna, who was prancing around in her new dress, blue eyes dancing, dark curls bouncing her multiple ribbon bows, as she introduced one family member after another to the new Christmas doll.

Things had begun to settle down a bit when Berta heard Aunt Cee whisper to her mother, "She gets prettier every day." Her eyes, filled with love and admiration, were on the tiny Glenna.

Her mother nodded. "Now if I can just manage to keep her sweet," she answered, her eyes misting.

"Glenna? I can't imagine her being anything but sweet. She's the kind that doesn't spoil. She loves to make people—happy. She—she just—bubbles."

Berta saw her mother nod.

Berta turned her eyes to the small Glenna. It was true. She bubbled. She—she glowed. And she did like to make people happy.

"I know a Chris'as song," she was informing her cousins and Uncle John. "You like to hear it?"

Oh, no, thought Berta. *She's gonna sing it all wrong again.*

She tried to put her hands over her ears as she hurried from the room, her storybook clutched in one arm.

She'd never get to show off how she could read. But suddenly she didn't care. She flung the book into the corner of the hallway and rushed up the stairs toward the little attic room where Grandmother kept the visitor's toy box. She wasn't anxious to play—but the room was the only haven she knew of where she would be left alone.

It wasn't so much that her little sister would sing the song all wrong, but the fact that the effort, no matter how poorly presented, would be acclaimed and applauded. That drove Berta to flee the coziness of Grandmother's Christmassy living room.

It was chilly in the unheated toy room. There was no warm fireplace ablaze with yule log. Shivering, Berta slumped down onto the rag rug that circled the floor. Her eyes turned to the big metal trunk holding all the dress-up things that Grandmother had given them to play with. She didn't feel like playing dress-up. Besides, it wasn't fun to play all alone. She wished Ada would come. She wished—she shivered again.

She slowly picked herself up from the floor and crossed to the window. Absentmindedly she began to scratch away at the frost on the pane. The cold made her fingers tingle, but she kept right on scratching—making the see-through spot grow bigger and bigger.

There was nothing to see when she finally could peep through. Just snow-covered fields and snow-covered bushes and a snow-covered road. She turned from the window, her shoulders slumped. Then a thought brought a smile to her face, a shine to her eyes.

I'm a helper, she thought. *Mama says so. I'll go down to the kitchen and help Granna.*

With quick steps she left the room. It would be good to get into the warmth of the kitchen—away from the chilling cold of the small attic room. It would be good to be a helper. To earn some of her grandmother's praise.

Suddenly Christmas Day looked much brighter.

She was breathless when she hurried into the kitchen, where her grandmother bent over an open oven removing a Christmas goose from the heat. Already Aunt Cee and Mama were there. Berta was sorry to see them, but she passed them by and stood before her grandmother.

"I came to help you, Granna," she said with pride.

Her grandmother looked up from the steaming goose and smiled.

"How nice," she responded. Then she added as she reached up to wipe her hand across her brow, "But I'm not sure the kitchen is the place for a pretty dress like you're wearing. You might splatter grease on it or—"

Berta's disappointment showed quickly on her face.

"But I might find a job for you," continued her grandmother. "Let's see. How about . . ." she hesitated as she looked around the kitchen. "I know. You can put some walnuts in that dish—for toasting after dinner."

It didn't sound like a very important job to Berta. Granna was lifting the goose onto a large platter. Mother was mashing creamy potatoes in a big kitchen kettle, and Aunt Cee was dishing vegetables into one of Granna's rose-colored bowls.

Berta looked down at her pretty dress. Glenna's Christmas dress had brought her nothing but praise, but her dress, with its ribbons and lace, had kept her from being a real helper. She didn't like the dress. She would never wear it again.

———

Carefully Berta pressed the cookie cutter into the rolled-out dough. Each press of the tin circle was placed with exactness. Mama said that it was important to learn how to do things right. Mama always praised effort.

"How are you doing?" asked her mother from her left.

"These are all done," answered Berta.

"Mine too," said Glenna.

Berta cast a quick glance toward the spot where Glenna worked beside her.

"Glenna," she said, exasperation edging her voice. "You did it all wrong. You cut cookies out of cookies. Look. That's not right. You're s'pose to put them side by side. Not over top."

Glenna looked up with hurt in her eyes.

"Mama," Berta turned to her mother, "you'll never be able to make them cook. They're all in small pieces."

"That's fine," said her mother, drawing near. "We can bake little cookie-pieces." She smiled.

Glenna's face brightened.

"But look—" whined Berta. "They're—chopped."

"Well . . . if we need to, we'll just roll the dough again," said her mother.

She leaned against the table and wiped her hands on the nearby towel as she surveyed the work of her youngest.

"Let's do that," she decided. "I'll roll the dough again and you can help Glenna cut the cookies."

"She don't know how," said Berta.

"That's why you'll teach her. You know how. You can show your sister."

"But *I'm* the helper," protested Berta.

She didn't like Glenna learning the things she had been taught. It meant that Glenna was butting in.

"Yes," answered her mother. "You are my big helper. But we—you and I—we need to teach Glenna how to help, too. She can be our little helper."

While she spoke, Mrs. Berdette was re-rolling the

cookie dough. Soon it was spread evenly before them.

"There now," she said, smiling at Berta. "You take Glenna's hand and help her cut some cookies."

Reluctantly Berta reached for the small hand. Glenna beamed at her big sister and allowed her hand to be guided for cut after cut.

"You see," said Berta, "you gotta place 'em beside. Not top of."

Glenna giggled.

"Now you cut one," ordered Berta.

Glenna reached her hand out to the cookie dough, her eyes still on Berta's face.

"No—not like that," cut in Berta sharply. "You're making it over top again."

Glenna jerked her attention back to the dough.

"Like this," said Berta, taking the small hand again.

Then she turned to her mother with an exasperated sigh.

"I don't think she's ever gonna learn right," she said with impatience. "I think I better be the only helper."

Her mother smiled.

"Just you wait and see," she responded with a little chuckle. "With you teaching your little sister, I'll have two good helpers before you know it."

Berta knew that the words were a compliment. She didn't quite understand them, but she suddenly felt important. She turned back to her little sister and helped the small hand press a new cut firmly into the dough spread out before them.

Chapter Four

School Days

Berta loved her little school in Allsburg. From the very first day she was a good scholar and came home each afternoon excited at the prospect of showing her mother what she had learned. Then it was a long, difficult wait until her father came home from work so she might proudly present her new knowledge to him as well. Both her mother and her father gave lavish praise as she read and recited and worked sums to show them how much she was learning. Soon she was encouraged to read bedtime stories to Glenna.

Glenna was a good listener, and Berta found herself enjoying her audience of one. Glenna's big blue eyes never left her sister's face as the story progressed. She pressed close against Berta's side, hanging on each turn of the new adventure.

Story-time extended to any time they could find some minutes together—from the moment Berta came bouncing in from her day of learning to the hour they were both sent off to bed. Glenna was always willing for a story, and Berta was more than ready to show off her skills.

Mrs. Berdette beamed at the pair of them, her expression showing her pride in Berta, her helper, who was so sweet as she entertained her little sister with the story hours. And Berta was such an apt student. Her reading skills could only benefit young Glenna, who was quickly developing a love for books as well—even though they were still childish tales.

The day came when Glenna joyously fell in step beside Berta and hippity-hopped her way down the short boardwalk to the farm lane that led to the road beyond. They turned to wave as Mrs. Berdette stood and watched the pair of them go. They didn't see the tears wiped heedlessly on the hem of her apron.

"You must listen carefully and obey," Berta was informing her younger sister. "You mustn't talk and you can't . . ."

The voice faded away into the distance. Glenna was still vigorously nodding her head to all Berta's instructions.

Glenna also turned out to be a very good student. She was quick to pick up the words in the books and before a year had passed was reading her own stories in the simple primers.

This was difficult for Berta. She missed the story hours. She missed Glenna, pushed up against her, her eyes growing larger as the action of the story unfolded.

One Thursday afternoon the girls came hurrying in from their classes without even passing into the kitchen to greet their mother and enjoy their cookies and milk. Over her shoulder Glenna told her mother she had a new primer and couldn't wait to read the stories. The two deposited their coats and lunch boxes on the corner table, and Berta took a seat on the settee while Glenna scrambled up beside her.

Berta held out her hand for the new book, but Glenna protectively moved it out of her reach.

"I'll read it," she said firmly.

"No, Glenna—let me read," argued Berta.

"But I want to read it myself," replied Glenna, her voice low.

"But I know more words than you," continued Berta.

"Teacher said I should practice," Glenna said with a shake of her curls. "An' I'm supposed to listen and obey."

Those had been Berta's instructions.

"You—you can practice—after," said Berta, not giving in.

"But I want to know what the stories say."

"I will read them to you. Then you'll know."

Glenna looked disappointed. "But I want to learn the surprise."

"What surprise?"

"The surprise at the end of the story."

Berta reached for the book. "You will learn the surprise when I read it. I'm bigger. I'm supposed to help you."

"I don't need your help anymore," Glenna asserted loudly, her book still held out of Berta's reach.

Berta made a dive for the book and grabbed it from Glenna's clutching hand. There was the sickening sound of paper tearing just as Mrs. Berdette entered the room from the kitchen to see what all the fuss was about.

"Girls!" she exclaimed, her eyes taking in the scene.

Glenna burst into tears at the sight of the damage to her new book.

Berta's eyes were filled with angry defiance. "She wouldn't let me read," she defended. "She hid her book—way over."

"I wanted to read it," cried Glenna. "I wanted to read it to myself."

"And look what has happened. A damaged book—that your father will need to pay for," scolded Mrs. Berdette, pointing to the torn page.

It was a sobering thought.

"And your teacher will be most disappointed that you have treated a book so," their mother went on. "And I am disappointed as well. I thought you both had learned how to care for books."

Glenna's blue eyes filled with tears of shame. Her book was torn; her mother was unhappy. Her father would be unhappy, too, and her teacher would most surely scold.

"It's Glenna's fault," said an angry and defiant Berta.

"Mama—I'm sorry," sobbed Glenna. "I'm sorry. I'll let Berta read. I promise," and she scooted down from the settee and ran to her mother, burying her face against the calico apron.

"Just a minute," said Mrs. Berdette, one hand resting on the young girl's shoulder. "I'm not sure Glenna should take the blame here."

Her eyes held Berta's. Berta lifted her chin, her dark eyes flashing.

"It *was* her fault," she argued.

Mrs. Berdette sat in a chair and moved the sobbing Glenna up against her knee.

"Now hush," she told the young child. "Hush—while we try to sort this out."

Glenna stood up, the sobs turning to noisy gulps as she wiped at tears with the backs of her hands.

"Now—let's start at the beginning," said her mother. "Whose book is it?"

No one spoke.

"Whose book?" she asked again.

At last Berta spoke. "Glenna's, but—"

Mrs. Berdette held up her hand. Berta refrained from speaking further.

"And Glenna wished to read her own book?" asked

Mrs. Berdette to clarify the point.

"I'm s'posed to read to her," declared Berta, her voice still showing her anger.

"I'm sorry," said Glenna in a shaky voice.

"Now wait," continued Mrs. Berdette. The two girls turned silent again.

"It was . . . very nice of you to read to Glenna, Berta. She has enjoyed listening to the stories that you read. But now she can read on her own. She doesn't need your help with the primers. She likes to discover what the words say—all by herself. Can you understand that?"

Berta refused to acknowledge the words of her mother. Mrs. Berdette turned back to the young Glenna. "So . . . because you wished to read the book yourself, you held the book away from Berta. Is that right?"

Glenna nodded slowly.

"She reached it way over," declared Berta hotly.

"So, because you wouldn't hand it over, Berta decided to grab it from you. Is that right?"

Glenna's big eyes filled with tears again.

"She wouldn't share," accused Berta.

"I didn't share," repeated Glenna, the tears spilling over.

"But—" began Mrs. Berdette, and for a moment she seemed at a loss to know how to continue. Finally she began slowly, "It's nice to share. It's what God wishes of us. He wants us to be . . . generous. Kind. Loving toward one another. But . . . but you don't always have to give what another demands. There are some . . . rights—of ownership. Rights that must be recognized. Do you understand?"

Neither girl nodded.

"Berta," Mrs. Berdette went on, "you were wrong to try to force the book away from your sister. It was her book. She was assigned to do the reading. You are responsible for causing the torn page. I expect your father may want to take the cost from your piggy bank."

Berta sat bolt upright. She had been hoarding every penny she was given. She hadn't yet decided what she wished to do with the money, but she had reveled in watching the little sum slowly grow.

"But it was Glenna—" she began.

Glenna was in tears. "I didn't share," she sobbed. "I didn't share my book and now—" The tears came too fast for her to continue. "I'll pay," she finally managed. "I'll pay, Mama."

"You don't even have money," an angry Berta flung at her younger sister. "You spend it all on candy."

"Then I'll—I'll—" Glenna could come up with no scheme to pay off the debt.

Mrs. Berdette rose to her feet, shaking her head, obviously not knowing what to do with the pair of them.

"I think you should both go to your room," she said quietly. "We'll need to sort this out later when your father comes home."

She returned to her supper preparations. After several moments had passed she peeked in on her two daughters. They were both curled up on Berta's bed, Glenna's dark hair fanned out over the white pillow, her deep blue eyes wide with fascination as Berta read to her from the torn first-grade primer.

———

Their father, after giving them both a stern talking-to, paid for the damage to the book. From then on, Glenna brought her new books home and dutifully—though somewhat mournfully—handed them to Berta for the first reading. Then she felt free to read the stories over and over to herself. But it wasn't quite the same.

She never got to discover the "surprise" in the story.

Berta secretly exulted. Her role had been firmly reestablished. She was the older. She was in charge.

———

"We need to hurry," urged Berta.

They were almost ready to leave for the Sunday morning service. Mrs. Berdette was making the final loops in Glenna's hair bow. Mr. Berdette had already left the house to hitch up the cutter, his heavy coat bundling him against the chill of the winter's morn.

Mrs. Berdette let her eyes travel to the mantel clock. "We have plenty of time," she responded.

"But we don't," chafed Berta. "We need to be there early. They are choosing parts for the Christmas play this morning."

"Well, I'm sure they won't make their choices before everyone gets there," said Mrs. Berdette.

"But they might. . . ." Berta's words trailed off. She had never yet been chosen for Mary. This year—*this year* she was determined to convince her teacher that she was the most suitable one for the part.

"I wanna be an angel," put in Glenna cheerily.

"You'd make a lovely angel," said Mrs. Berdette, a smile tilting her lips.

Berta cast a cross look at the two of them. Glenna, with her frills and bows, smiled up into the face of her mother. Berta tossed her short hair. She didn't want frills and bows. She insisted on plain dresses. She didn't even want lace on her shirtwaists. At first her mama had quietly argued, but at last she had conceded. Berta noticed that her mother seemed to take special delight in sewing pretty things for Glenna.

Berta kicked her toe against the table leg. If they

didn't hurry she'd be sure to lose the part.

By the time Mrs. Berdette had helped Glenna with her coat and muff and buttoned her own coat firmly about her slim form, Mr. Berdette was at the door with the cutter and team.

Berta tried to get Glenna to settle quickly as she tucked the blankets closely about them to ward off the cold.

The horses snorted and tossed their heads, puffs of frosty breath making little clouds that traveled up the front of their long faces.

At last they were on their way. Berta ached to tell her papa to hurry the team—but she knew it wouldn't work. He did not like to run the team in cold weather. He did not wish them to be sweaty when he tied them to the hitching rail and threw the coarse blankets over their broad backs. They had to wait in the cold until the service ended.

"I bet they'll be all chosen," Berta grumbled to herself.

But when they arrived at the little church, others were still pulling into the yard. Mothers and children were delivered to the steps while fathers or older sons drove on to tie the horses to the hitching rails.

Berta didn't even call greetings to her church friends. She was fearful that if she acknowledged them the teachers might notice their appearance and consider one of them for the cherished role.

Heavy coats were hung on pegs by the door and children were bustled off to the small side room where parts were being decided.

"Let's all sit down," said elderly Mrs. Twing. She had been doing the Christmas program just forever.

The children obediently took seats. Wishing to be noticed, Berta made sure she was in the front row.

"Let's begin with the shepherds."

Three junior boys were chosen for the shepherds. Another three were picked for the wise men. Four pre-schoolers beamed as they were designated as sheep.

"We'll need an angel choir," said Mrs. Twing, "but we'll leave that for last. Anyone without a speaking part will be in the choir. It's very important that we have a good choir."

Berta understood the words in spite of Mrs. Twing's effort to hide the meaning. The angel choir would simply be the leftovers. Berta did not want that.

"We need an innkeeper."

Mrs. Twing's eyes traveled over the three older boys who sat on the very last row trying hard to look inconspicuous in spite of red faces and jabbing elbows.

"Carl? How about being the innkeeper?"

Carl reddened and was poked in the ribs from each side. He managed to nod.

Berta watched. She had hoped with all her heart that Mrs. Twing would choose Carl for Joseph. Secretly she liked Carl.

"The angel Gabriel," said Mrs. Twing. "Luke—you would make a good Gabriel."

It was Luke's turn to blush.

Berta squirmed. Only one older boy was left. Thomas Hawkins. She didn't like Thomas Hawkins. She would hate playing Mary with him as Joseph. She wanted to protest. She almost raised her hand. But Mrs. Twing was continuing.

"Now—all we have left are Joseph and Mary. Let's see. Thomas—you will be our Joseph." Mrs. Twing stopped and cast her eyes over the row of older girls. Berta squirmed. It seemed to take forever before Mrs. Twing spoke again.

"Oh, my. This is a very hard decision. We have so

many fine choices for Mary. Let's see. Oh, my. Well . . ."

Berta wriggled on her seat.

"Berta would make a good Mary." It was Glenna who spoke up, her childish voice trembling with her excitement, her blue eyes shining.

"Yes," said Mrs. Twing, "yes—Berta would make a fine Mary, I'm sure."

Berta breathed in deeply. She was in.

But Mrs. Twing was continuing to speak. "This year, though, I think—yes—this year it will be Emelia's turn. She has not yet been Mary, and this is her last year in our program."

Berta felt the breath leave her lungs and the hot flush of anger stain her cheeks. It wasn't fair. Emelia would make an—an *ugly* Mary. It would be all wrong. Her bright red hair and freckled face would not go at all well with the blue robe and white head veil. She would make an awful Mary. The whole play would be all wrong. It wasn't fair. It just wasn't fair.

Berta dipped her head. She knew all eyes must be upon her. They would all know that she had been slighted. They would—

Berta lifted her eyes again. To her surprise they were not all looking at her. They did not even seem to notice her discomfort. Only one pair of eyes was studying her face—the blue eyes of her little sister, Glenna. Such agony—such sympathy—showed in Glenna's eyes that Berta felt even angrier.

"And the rest of you," Mrs. Twing was saying, "will be our special angel choir. You—"

"I won't," shouted Berta, jumping up from the bench where she sat. "An angel is no part at all. It's just a—a—"

But she could not go on. Her voice choked up with her anger. She wanted to cry but she refused to give them the satisfaction of seeing that they had wounded her.

Mrs. Twing's eyes opened wide with surprise and shock.

"Why, Berta—" she began but seemed not to know what else to say.

In the back row the big boys were tittering.

Berta stood her ground. She crossed her arms in front of her and shook her head with each angry word. "I won't be an angel. Glenna can be your angel. I'm not a little kid anymore. I won't be an angel."

She cast a disdainful glance toward Emelia. "An' Mary doesn't have red hair," she said with emphasis.

"Berta," said Mrs. Twing firmly. "Berta—sit down."

Berta tilted her chin stubbornly.

"Sit down," the words came again.

She had to do it. She knew that—but, oh, how it rankled to give in. She plopped down on the bench, making it quiver with her forcefulness. Her arms were still crossed in front of her, her face was tipped forward so that her hair almost covered the crimson of her flushed cheeks.

"I think you and I need to have a talk," said Mrs. Twing. "Mrs. Lawlor, will you take over the class, please?"

The "talk" did not result in a change in the assigned parts. It did result in a further talk in the Berdette household.

Berta sang with the angel choir—but inwardly she hated the assignment. Glenna tried to cheer her by telling her "how pretty" she looked in the white flannel robe and "how nice" she sang the songs.

Berta took no comfort from Glenna's compliments. Outwardly she performed as she had been bidden by her father. Inwardly she protested with every breath she took.

But the words of her mother lingered in the back of her mind to trouble her.

"Oh, Berta. I don't know what to do with you. I fear what that defiant spirit and quick temper might cost you in life."

Chapter Five

Teen Years

Anxious footsteps awakened Berta from a sound sleep. She lifted her head from the pillow and listened. She could hear the troubled voices that drifted down the hall, but she could not understand the words.

She sat up and swung her feet to the area rug beside her bed. It was still dark outside. Something strange was going on.

She looked over at her younger sister. Berta could see her faint outline beneath the bulk of Granna's pieced quilt. Glenna still slept on.

Stealthily, so as not to awaken Glenna, she moved toward the door, her white flannel nightgown swishing about her bare ankles.

There was a light on in the living room. She could see its faint glow from the hallway. She moved toward the light, wondering what had brought her folks from their beds at such an unearthly hour.

She stepped to the door of the room and was shocked to see the doctor. No one was sick.

Then her eyes moved to Pastor Jenkins, the minister of their small church, sitting on the settee, his hand sympathetically placed on the robed arm of her mother. A strange fear gripped Berta's heart.

Berta took a step into the room. Three heads lifted. Three pairs of eyes fastened on her face. She could tell her mother had been crying.

"What is it?" Berta managed to ask. "What's happened?"

"Oh, Berta," sobbed her mama, and she extended a hand toward the young girl.

Berta moved quickly to her and knelt in front of her, one hand going to her mother's dampened cheek. "What happened?" she repeated, but her mother was unable to answer because of the sobs that shook her body.

It was the minister who spoke. "Your father," he said slowly, sadly.

Berta's head jerked up, her eyes wide with fear. "What?" she asked. "What has happened?"

"It was a heart attack," responded the doctor, sympathy deepening his voice. "We were unable to save him."

"You mean—?" began Berta, looking from one drawn face to another. She couldn't finish the sentence. Would not even allow herself to finish the thought.

Pastor Jenkins nodded. "I'm sorry. So sorry," he said. "He's gone."

Berta stood quickly to her feet. It wasn't true. It couldn't be true. She had seen her father just a few short hours before. They had spent the afternoon tramping through the meadow by the creek searching for leaf specimens for her biology class. He was fine. Just fine. There was some mistake.

She looked again at her mother. The woman was still weeping. Berta knelt again by her side and took her hand in both her own.

"Mama?" Her one word was a question. A plea.

Her mother reached out to her and placed her hands

on each side of her face. The anguish in her mother's eyes answered the question for her. It was true. It was real. They had lost her father. Berta buried her face in her mother's lap and wept unashamedly.

What would they ever do without him?

Her thoughts went on. He had been so much more than a father. He had been her friend, her encourager, her constant source of love and acceptance. Whatever would she do without him?

———

Somehow the two girls and their mother made it through the difficult days that followed. Somehow they stood by the open grave as the last words were spoken by Pastor Jenkins. Somehow—somehow—they made it through the first agonizing weeks, the months—that eventually stretched into a year. They clung together. Sharing—yet keeping secret thoughts from one another.

They discovered that life went on. They even managed to establish some sort of daily routine to replace the familiar. The girls continued on with their schooling on weekdays. Their mother spent her time in baking, sewing—family chores. But Berta felt that the glow had left her mother's cheeks, the light had left her eyes. She wondered just how often her pillow was soaked with tears after she retired to an empty bedroom at the end of the day.

Glenna was their one bit of sunshine. In spite of her own pain, she found little ways to bring some joy and laughter into the otherwise somber household. At length, even their mother managed to laugh again.

But Berta found it hard to laugh. Though she never would have said so, she was angry. Angry with life—and even angrier at death. What right had death to steal away her father? To destroy their happy home? Berta buried her thoughts deep inside and lifted a stubborn chin. Her father had been a good man. Unselfish. Giving. Seeking to fulfil God's command to love and serve others. Perhaps it didn't pay. What good had it done him?

Berta would never have expressed her angry thoughts, but inwardly she gave them room to grow. She had no intention of standing idly by and letting anyone, or anything, take from her what she deserved. Nor would she bear pain simply because she couldn't fight back. No one was going to rally to the aid of a passive soul, she decided. She would fight on her own behalf. She would look after her own interests.

———

"May I walk you home?"

It was Thomas Hawkins who stood before her. Berta lowered her gaze. It wasn't that Thomas Hawkins was difficult to look at. He had really grown into a very nice-looking young man. Berta had found herself stealing frequent glances his way.

And he was—well, pleasant as well. Berta could not deny the fact. Thomas Hawkins had been favorably impressing her for many months. Had been impressing several of her classmates too. A number of the girls were whispering their feelings concerning Thomas Hawkins.

But Berta was surprised that Thomas Hawkins had noticed her. Why her—among all her attractive school friends? Why was he asking to walk her home from class?

She flushed. She wasn't sure how she should answer.

"I—I need to hurry," she said at last. "Mama needs me."

"We'll walk fast," he countered lightly.

But Berta shook her head.

"I have to get right home. Mama needs my help."

It was the truth—stretched to an untruth. She did assist her mother with household chores and yard work. But her mama would not be standing at the door, anxiously awaiting her arrival.

"Some other time, then," said Thomas, and he smiled, nodded pleasantly, and turned to go.

Berta gathered her books, her face still flushed. *Why is Thomas asking to walk me home?* she puzzled again. Why—when there were so many other girls to choose from? Like pixie-faced Matilda, or hazel-eyed Violet, or pert Mary Jane.

She was—she was just plain *Berta*. Her dark hair, now grown long to please Mama, was pinned back tightly in a simple roll at the base of her neck. With her severe skirts and plain shirtwaists, devoid of even ribbons and lace, she was the unfeminine one—it didn't make sense. Was it a dare? Was it meant as an embarrassment? Was it simply to get close to the bubbling Glenna? All the schoolboys seemed to have a crush on young Glenna, who just smiled her sweet smile and treated them all as big brothers. Was this Thomas's way of trying to break out of the pack of Glenna's admirers and get some extra attention?

Berta lifted a stubborn chin into the air and headed for home. She would not allow Thomas to make her the laughingstock of her entire class. She would rebuff him before he had the chance.

"You dropped something."

Berta did not recognize the masculine voice that spoke softly behind her, but she knew he was speaking to her. She turned and looked into a pair of deep brown eyes.

He smiled.

Berta let her gaze travel over his face. He was new. She had never seen him in church before.

She felt her face flush.

"Here," he said, smiling slightly. "You dropped this."

Berta let her eyes fall to the clean white square of cotton that he held in his outstretched hand. Her hankie. The flush on her face deepened. He would think she had deliberately dropped it in an effort to get his attention. It was a familiar trick of young ladies and one he was sure to be aware of.

"I—I—" she began but didn't know quite how to continue. Then her pride took over and she lifted her chin in defiance. "I did not drop it intentionally," she declared stoutly. "I was not even aware that you were about."

Surprise registered on his face—but then he smiled. "Touché," he said with a chuckle. "I'm sure you didn't."

Berta stood her ground, her armful of Sunday school materials held tightly against her white shirtwaist.

"However," said the young man, still appearing amused, "you may claim it if you wish."

Berta flushed. She reached out and took the hankie from him and spun on her heel. With head held high she marched on to the small room where her class of primary students awaited her Sunday morning instruction.

But it was not easy to collect her thoughts. She kept seeing the amused brown eyes. The cleft in the strong chin. The sun-browned smooth cheeks that she somehow realized had been newly shaven. For the first time in her young life, Berta was smitten.

———

His name was Parker Oliver. He was the son of the man who had purchased a local hotel. All the girls were swooning over him. Even Thomas Hawkins was no longer the frontrunner for feminine interest. Berta watched it all from a distance. She pretended she did not even know that he existed—that her pulse did not quicken each time he made an appearance.

She lifted her head just a bit higher whenever she passed by him. For the first time in her life she was tempted to put just a bit of lace on her Sunday shirtwaists. To pin her hair a tiny bit looser, letting tendrils curl about her oval face.

She flushed and chided herself and straightened her back to strengthen her resolve.

But her resolve weakened each time he sent a smile her way. Each item in his Sunday wardrobe, each mannerism, each word he spoke in her hearing, was duly noted.

But she pretended not to pay any attention.

And then the inevitable happened.

"Mama," Glenna called before she had even closed the door behind her. "Oh, Mama—you'll never guess! Parker has asked me to the corn roast. Oh—can I go, Mama? Please—please, say yes." And Glenna threw herself at her mother's knee.

"Wait—" said her mother, and then managed a silvery laugh. "What's this all about, child?"

"Parker. Oh, Mama—he is—is just divine. And he asked me to the corn roast. Oh—I'll just—just—weep if you don't let me go."

Mrs. Berdette smiled. "Well—I'm thankful you didn't use the annoying expression that you would just 'die'," she responded.

"Well—I might do that too," said Glenna, bringing another laugh from her mother.

"Oh, I doubt that anything so dreadful as that would happen," teased Mrs. Berdette.

"Please, can I go? It's well chaperoned. It's a church party. Please, Mama."

No one had looked Berta's direction. No one had seen her face turn ashen. No one noticed the pain darkening her eyes.

She rose silently to her feet and moved toward the door while Glenna still babbled on in coaxing tone, trying to convince her mother that she was not too young to attend the youth corn roast with an escort.

"You're not yet fifteen," Mrs. Berdette argued, but Berta thought she didn't sound too firm in her position.

"Everyone says I look and act at least sixteen," Glenna was informing her mother as Berta stole from the room.

Berta would not have denied the fact. Glenna *was* mature for her age. But Parker? Parker was nearing twenty. Berta had slyly wrangled the information from his kid sister. Did he really wish to attend with the young Glenna?

Yes. Yes of course he did.

All the boys wished to win the attention of her delightful sister. All the girls were secretly jealous of her—yet couldn't keep from liking her, no matter how hard they tried. Berta knew that. Glenna was just—just Glenna. There was nothing about Glenna that one could dislike or disapprove of. She had always been that way. Always would be.

Hurt and anger swept through Berta. For one awful minute she wished she were an only child, that her mother had never blessed her with a baby sister. Not a sister . . . like Glenna.

"What should I wear? Oh, I don't know which to choose. This one or this one? What do you think?"

Mama had given Glenna permission to attend the corn roast. Excitedly she went through her closet, trying to decide on a gown that would fit her mother's demand for sensible, warm attire, but would still favorably impress the amazing Parker.

Berta chose not to be involved. She kept her nose in her book and tried to shut out the sound of Glenna's voice.

"What do you think?" Glenna asked again.

When there was still no response, she crossed to where Berta sat propped up by the pillows on her bed.

"What do you think, Berta?" she asked at close range.

Berta could no longer ignore her.

"How should I know," she replied tersely.

Glenna's large eyes showed surprise.

"And what do I care?" Berta shifted her weight to a more comfortable position.

"But—" began Glenna.

Berta only stared at her book.

"Aren't you going?" asked Glenna, her voice full of shock as it dawned on her that Berta was not preparing for the occasion.

"No!" said Berta flatly.

"But Thomas asked—"

Berta gave her a sharp look. She wondered how Glenna knew about Thomas's invitation.

"So—?" she said haughtily.

"He'll be—hurt," went on Glenna timidly.

"So who made you Thomas's guardian?" demanded Berta, straightening up against the pillows. "And what business is it of yours, anyway?"

"Well—none, but—"

"Then stay out of it," snapped Berta.

Glenna blinked.

"Okay," she finally nodded. "I didn't mean to—to pry. I just thought—"

"Well, don't."

Glenna moved away from the bed and began to quietly change into the gown of her choice. As she pinned up her hair and tucked in stray curls she dared to speak again.

"I think Thomas is nice," she said carefully.

"Then why don't you go with him?" Berta responded harshly.

"Because Parker asked me," Glenna replied, casting a glance Berta's way. Then she stopped short at the look on Berta's face before the older girl could hide it.

"Oh, Berta," she exclaimed, her voice full as the truth dawned. For one moment she stood in silence, studying the face of her older sister. Then she said, "Do you like him?"

Berta fought for proper control. Her chin lifted and she stared evenly back at Glenna. "What do you mean?" she asked as matter-of-factly as she could.

"Parker? Do you like Parker? Because if you—"

So here it was. Glenna—generous Glenna—was going to be "giving" again. She was going to offer Parker to her older sister—to keep the peace—to present happiness. It was a generous offer. The most generous that Glenna had ever made. But—even if she was willing to make the sacrifice, didn't Parker have some say in the matter? Would he be willing to be "handed off"? Certainly not. Not to the plainest girl in the school.

"Don't be ridiculous," retorted Berta. "Are you out of your mind? I think boys are nothing but—offensive bores."

Glenna drew in her breath. "I'm glad," she admitted. "Really glad. I like him—a lot."

Chapter Six

Changes

The cold fall wind sent shivers through Berta's slender frame, making her pull her long gray coat closer about her body and hurry her step. She had graduated from high school and taken a job at the town library.

She was thankful for the job. It provided a bit of income to supplement her father's insurance money provided by the bank where he had put in the years of his employment. And it also gave her opportunity to be among books.

Berta had never lost her love for books. She found it difficult to resist the urge to bury herself in one when duty called her to be filing them back on the shelf instead. But she did borrow—extensively—and at night, as her daily tasks were completed, she pulled a chair close to the warmth of the fire and drank from the exciting pages.

She would have been quite pleased with her life— were it not for one nagging concern that gnawed at her and grew with her own maturity and ability to assess her mother's condition. Mrs. Berdette really was not her normal self. Had not seemed to be strong ever since they had lost their father.

Berta watched her carefully, daily measuring her listlessness and lack of energy.

She knew that her mother tried to hide her state of health. She never talked about it if Berta brought the subject up. "I'm fine," she would argue defensively, and then try a light laugh. "Remember, I'm not as young as I once was," she would add.

But Berta knew that was not the reason. Her mother was still young. Not nearly old enough to be troubled by symptoms of old age.

Others did not think she was old either. Mr. Mills, the bachelor hardware owner, asked her permission to call, and his request was firmly declined. Mr. Willows, a widower farmer, had offered his services as a handyman along with his attention—and that, also, was rejected.

Berta knew her mother remained a young, attractive woman. Her excuses of age did not account for her pale face or slow step.

But there seemed to be little that Berta could do— little besides worrying and watching.

Berta drew near the library, moving quickly. The bitter wind had her shivering in spite of the warmth of her coat.

She had to tug against the strength of the wind to get the door to agree to being opened. Making a blustery entrance, she thrust her body through the opening and pulled the door quickly closed behind her.

"My—it's nasty out," she commented as she shook the snow from the scarf she had worn over her hair.

Miss Phillips, the middle-aged woman who shared the responsibility of the town library with her, looked up from the records before her.

"Did you walk?" she asked absently.

Berta nodded. It was much easier to walk the distance than to worry about the team.

"Have you thought about moving into Allsburg?" The woman surprised Berta by her question. Miss Phillips was usually quiet and withdrawn.

"Oh my, no," Berta quickly replied. "Mama needs me."

"I didn't mean you alone. I meant your family," the woman went on. "I know your mother rents her land—but the place still must be a burden."

Berta wanted to argue. Her father had not really been a farmer—though he had insisted on owning a bit of land just beyond the edge of town. "A gentleman farmer," he had jokingly referred to himself. He insisted that he needed a bit of diversion from his banking duties. A way to get exercise. A place to keep his fine team of bays. But now that her father was gone, the bays were really more nuisance than they were assistance. Neither she nor her mother appreciated the task of hitching the team to the buggy or cutter. They even walked to church when the weather permitted—and when the weather was inclement, the Morgans kindly offered them a ride.

"I'm sure Mama would not like to leave our country home," Berta responded, but the idea lingered with her as she went about her tasks of the day.

The cold wind and drifting snow kept most patrons from venturing out to the library. Berta found the day dragging until she was informed by the older woman that she might as well choose a book and settle herself for a good read. From then on the day sped by on swift wings. Berta was sorry to see it come to an end.

"Do you think you should spend the night in town with friends?" the woman asked as Berta buttoned on her coat and tied her scarf firmly around her head.

"Oh, I could never do that. Mama would worry. Someone would need to get word to her—and I might as well be the one," she finished with a little smile.

Miss Phillips nodded, then hastened to add, "Well, I do think it is too far to be walking in such weather. You must make arrangements with your mother that on such wintry days you'll stay in town."

Then Miss Phillips seemed to bite her tongue and turned sharply away as though she had already said much more than she had intended.

Berta nodded. She'd have to do some thinking about their situation. It was a long way for Glenna to be walking to school as well. Perhaps they would be better off in town.

By the time Berta had made her way through the swirling snow and reached the Berdette doorstep, it was getting quite dark out. She was glad to lift the latch and press her way into the warmth of the front hallway.

"I was concerned," her mother said, a worried look on her face. "It's so stormy."

Berta replied by shivering and asking, "Is Glenna home?"

"Parker brought her. He picked her up at school. He offered to go back for you, but I knew you wouldn't be able to leave until your hours—"

"That's all right," Berta interrupted. She certainly wouldn't have enjoyed a trip home through the storm with Glenna's Parker.

The two were now seeing each other regularly. They were recognized as an established couple—both at the little church and also in the community. Folks had long since stopped making comments about "how young Glenna is to have a steady beau."

But even though Berta also accepted Parker being in love with her little sister, she still struggled with the fact that she found him very attractive.

"Miss Phillips told me not to come in the morning if the storm persists," she told her mother. "No one ventures out to the library in such weather anyway."

Mrs. Berdette nodded. "I have some tea ready," she told Berta and led the way into the living room and the warm fire blazing in the open fireplace.

Berta extended her hands. She hadn't realized just how cold she was until the warmth of the room surrounded her.

"I'll need to get out to the horses," she murmured as she accepted the cup of tea from her mother.

There were also the chickens to care for and the two cows that remained from her father's livestock.

"Glenna is doing the chores," replied her mother.

"Glenna?" Delicate Glenna was mucking around in the barns?

"She knew you'd be chilled clear through," Mrs. Berdette went on.

Berta took her tea to a nearby chair. "Mama," she said, pushing some stray locks back from her face. Usually her hair was so severely tucked and pinned that it didn't dare break free of its knot at the nape of her neck, but the strong wind had dislodged it. "Miss Phillips made an interesting comment. She suggested that we move into town."

Berta waited for her words to sink in. She expected her mother to respond quickly with strong opposition. But there was silence in the room.

Berta looked up from her teacup to see her mother rubbing her hands together as though in agitation. At last she spoke.

"I've been thinking the same myself," she said to a surprised Berta. "It doesn't make sense for you and Glenna to walk to and fro—especially in such weather."

Berta stared at her mother, hardly believing her ears.

"Glenna will be done with school in the spring," continued her mother slowly, "and I've an idea that Parker will not wish to wait long for a wedding. The farm . . ."

But Berta did not hear her next words. She was in shock with the calm way that her mother had spoken of Glenna—little Glenna. Surely she wasn't ready to get married. Parker's *wife*?

Berta shook her head to clear it. The room seemed to be spinning around her.

"Are you all right?" she heard her mother asking.

Berta jerked back to attention.

"I'm fine. Just fine," she insisted. "I—I was just—thinking—I mean—it took me by surprise—your speaking of—of Glenna and—I mean—I guess I still think of her as—as a child."

Her mother smiled. "I'd like to think of her in that way, too," she said slowly. "But I . . . I keep seeing the love in her young man's eyes."

"But she's only seventeen," argued Berta setting aside her teacup.

"I was married at her age," answered her mother softly.

Berta could not hide her surprise. She had known that fact—but she had never before thought about it in relation to an *actual age*—her sister's age. Her mother seemed so—so different from her little sister.

They both sat silently, each deep in her own thoughts. It was Berta who finally spoke.

"So there will just be me—and you," she stated.

Mrs. Berdette stirred. She moistened her lips and started to speak, then shifted uncomfortably. Fear gripped Berta's heart. Was her mother hiding a secret? Had she, without confiding, agreed to the proposal of one of her male acquaintances?

"Have you made plans without—?" Berta stopped.

She was challenging her mother's right to make her own decisions. There was more than concern in her voice. There was also annoyance.

"Well . . . not really. I mean, I haven't decided . . . I've just been . . . thinking." She stirred again as though hesitant to go on.

"About what?" prompted Berta.

Her mother seemed to take courage. She took a deep breath and plunged ahead, not meeting Berta's dark eyes. "Your grandmother has asked me to move in with her. She isn't as strong as she once was. Uncle John would be greatly relieved if I'd agree to the arrangement. He's been advising me to sell our small farm—get rid of the nuisance of livestock—the hens—the team. He thinks—"

Berta breathed a deep sigh of relief. She was glad her mother didn't plan to remarry. She wouldn't have liked another man to take her father's place.

"And what am I to do?" she asked more sharply than she intended. "With you at Granna's and Glenna married—what happens to me?"

It wasn't fair. Her accusation of desertion hung heavily in the room between them even though she had not really spoken the words.

"That—that is why I haven't made a decision," her mother hurriedly tried to explain.

"So—" said Berta rising from her chair and crossing to stare down at the burning log in the fireplace. "I am the hindrance to your—plans? I—"

"Berta," spoke her mother with a sob in her voice. "You are no hindrance. You are—"

Berta felt a hand on her arm and knew that her mother stood close beside her. She knew there would be tears in her mother's eyes. Well, so be it. It wasn't fair. It wasn't fair at all that they had been planning—the two

of them—planning how they would change their lives—
how they would move on—and just leave her to—to muddle her own way through it all.

"Berta," said her mother again, pleadingly. "No one
has made plans—yet. We need to talk about it. Decide.
We need to do what is best—for all of us."

Her voice sounded choked. Berta was afraid her
mother was going to weep.

"I need to think," Berta stated, pulling away from her
mother's hand, and she left for the bedroom she still
shared with Glenna.

In her severe agitation Berta wished she had a room
of her own. Some place of privacy. Some place of quiet.
She hoped with all her heart that Glenna would not come
bursting in, her cheeks flushed by the chilling wind, her
eyes sparkling with memories of her ride home with
Parker.

Berta buried her face in her pillow and closed her
eyes. She had to think. But she didn't want to think. She
had to get back control. But she had never had control.
Not really. They had fooled her. She had thought that
with Father gone she was now in charge of the family.
But they had been making plans—all along—secretly.
Plans that did not even include her. She ached with the
desire to cry. To scream out against the world that always
seemed to hurt her.

But she did not cry. She refused to. She just lay there
in her silence, aching and angry.

At last she rose and pushed her pillow firmly to where
it belonged on her bed.

"All right," she said aloud as she straightened her
shoulders. "If they don't need me—I don't need them either. They can make their plans. From now on I'll make
plans to suit myself. They can go their way—I'll go mine.
And I'll do just fine—without them."

Chapter Seven

Parker

Supper was a quiet meal. Even Glenna, who usually chattered happily, seemed to sense the mood of the two others at the table and was unusually subdued and pensive. For her part, Berta had made a personal decision. She would let things continue as they were until Glenna had finished her school year, and then she would make her own plans. Perhaps Miss Phillips would know of a room where she could board. Surely the salary that she made at her job would cover the rent. She would no longer need to be paying toward the support of her family.

Mrs. Berdette, too, seemed to be miles away. *What are her thoughts?* Berta wondered, but she did not ask. Did not even enter into conversation beyond "Pass the butter, please."

In spite of the continued fury of the storm, Parker came to call. Berta lifted her eyes from the pages of the book she had brought from the library. She saw Glenna's eager greeting and Parker's ready response. With heavy heart she realized that her mother was likely right.

Parker was sure to be asking for Glenna's hand before many months passed.

"Good evening," Parker addressed her politely.

Berta was sure he had no idea how his solicitude set her heart to racing.

Don't be a fool, she scolded herself. *He is Glenna's beau.*

She managed to answer his comments without giving away her true feelings, and then when she felt she had exchanged enough conversation to be seen as not running away, she excused herself.

"Oh, don't go. Stay and chat," invited Glenna.

Berta indicated the book in her hand. "I am at a most interesting spot." She managed a slight smile. "I'm afraid I can't wait to see just how it will turn out."

"But we don't want to drive you away from the warm fire," spoke Parker. "Glenna and I will be happy to visit in the kitchen if—"

"No. No, that's not necessary. I have a warm robe— and slippers. I'll not miss the fire."

And Berta hastened to leave the room before they could protest further.

"I think I'll retire early," she heard her mother saying. "It's been a long day. I find I am quite weary."

Berta paused in her departure. She wasn't sure that it was proper to leave the young girl and her suitor alone in the living room.

"I'll not be staying late," assured Parker.

Berta hurried on down the hall.

The book had lost its fascination. She flipped through the pages, hardly understanding what she was reading. At last she tossed it aside and began her preparations for retiring.

Before she could even climb between the cozy flannel

sheets she heard Glenna humming her way down the hall.

As she entered the room her eyes turned to Berta. "Shall I bank the fires?" she asked.

That had always been Berta's job.

"Parker gone already?" asked Berta rather than answering.

"He thought it best," responded Glenna, then followed with, "He always frets about my reputation. It's so sweet."

Berta said nothing.

"Do you wish me to bank the fire?" Glenna asked again.

"No, I will," replied Berta and slipped her feet back into her slippers and tied her heavy robe close about her.

"Mama is already sleeping. I peeked in on her," said Glenna.

Berta looked up. She nodded.

"Berta—is something wrong with Mama?"

Berta looked at her younger sister evenly. "Why do you ask?"

"Well . . . I—I don't know. She just seems—worried. Preoccupied."

"I—I guess she has a lot on her mind," responded Berta as she moved toward the door.

"Like what?" asked Glenna frankly.

Berta turned to look at her. There was no way she was going to say to Glenna that their mother expected her to soon receive a proposal of marriage from her gentleman caller. Nor was she prepared to say that she intended to move out on her own at her earliest opportunity. Instead she said, "Granna isn't doing well on her own. Uncle John thinks Mama should move in with her."

Glenna stared.

"Why haven't I been told?" she asked.

"I hadn't been told either," Berta shot back. "Until to-night. Mama told me just before you came in from chor-ing."

"So that's why the silence," mused Glenna.

Berta nodded.

"So we are to stay on here alone?" continued Glenna.

"No. No—the farm will be sold."

"Sold?" Glenna sounded incredulous.

Berta nodded.

"But that's—it was Papa's pride. He—"

"It only makes sense," Berta said. "It's ridiculous for us to be tending cows and chickens and a team we never use."

She moved toward the door again.

Again Glenna stopped her. "Are we all to live with Granna, then?"

"Please, Glenna," said Berta in exasperation. "I don't have the answers. I don't even know what Mama is going to decide to do. It all will need to be worked out when—when the time comes."

Glenna looked like she was about to cry. She dipped her head quickly and when she looked back up she was biting her lip and blinking her long dark lashes.

"I hate change," she whispered. "I hate it. It is so—so unsettling."

Berta turned away.

You have no idea just how unsettling it will be, she thought to herself. *But you'll be the lucky one.*

———

At least three times a week Parker came to call. All through the winter months and on into the spring he ap-peared at their front door, hat in his hand. Three times a week Berta excused herself from the room and went to the kitchen to sew or to her bedroom to read.

The pain had grown less with the quiet knowledge that what her mama had said was surely true. Parker would one day—soon—be Glenna's husband. Berta trained herself to think of the young man that way.

But he still had little ways of unknowingly bringing her sorrow. Like the time he brought her a simple bouquet of fresh spring lilacs. And the time he returned from a trip with a lace-trimmed hankie.

"I thought maybe you had lost all your others," he quipped, reminding her of their first introduction.

Berta flushed.

Parker was always doing thoughtful little things for their mother as well. He took her for Sunday outings along with Glenna. He offered to take Berta along too, but she always found some reason to be excused.

And he brought fancy chocolates and colorful cottons for embroidery work and even little jokes and amusing stories that he clipped from newspapers. It would have been hard for Mrs. Berdette to find anything wrong with Parker Oliver.

"I would like the pleasure of taking my three favorite ladies out for dinner next Saturday night," Parker announced one Thursday as he was about to take his leave.

Glenna flushed her pleasure, the deep dimple showing in each cheek.

Mrs. Berdette looked up from her sewing, her eyes taking on a special shine.

"That would be lovely. Thank you," she replied.

Parker turned his eyes to Berta.

"I—I'm not sure. I might—"

"Please," Parker surprised her by pleading. "I would so much like it to be a family dinner."

And you fully intend to put an end to our family, was her unspoken retort.

"Please, Berta," begged Glenna, moving up beside her and slipping an arm around her waist. "Please—this once."

"I'll . . . see," said Berta.

That was as close to a promise as she would come.

Try as she might, Berta could find no good reason to refuse to accompany the family to the local hotel for dinner. She both looked forward to a night out and dreaded the event.

He's going to ask Mama for permission to marry, I just know it, she told herself. *Glenna finishes school next month.*

Parker's buggy drew up to the front hitching rail promptly at six, the agreed time, and the three ladies were at the door ready to meet him. He let his gaze travel from one to another.

"How lovely you look," he said with sincerity, including more than Glenna in his comment. "I will be the envy of every gentleman in town tonight."

Glenna smiled on her mother and sister and took Parker's proffered arm. "You tease," she laughed, "but we love it."

Each lady was carefully handed up into the buggy, and then they were off. In spite of her dark mood, Berta found herself enjoying the drive into town.

They were escorted into the hotel dining room by the attendant and seated at a table with fine white linen and gleaming silver.

"My," exclaimed Mrs. Berdette in appreciation, "I wasn't aware that we had such elegant dining in our town. It's been years since I've sat at such a table."

Parker did not bother to explain that he had made

special arrangements at his father's hotel.

Berta's eyes grew larger with each course of the meal. *What an awful lot of trouble to go to just to impress a girl's family before asking for her hand in marriage,* she thought to herself. *Well, it will do little to sway me.*

And she steeled herself for what she was sure would come.

But the evening continued with no mention made of upcoming wedding plans. Parker included all three of them in his lively conversation, bringing laughter with his amusing tales and good-humored comments.

The evening passed much more quickly than any of the three would have liked. Before she knew it, Berta was being escorted from the dining room with its glowing candles and reflecting mirrors.

"This has been a delightful evening," Mrs. Berdette exclaimed sincerely.

"We must do it again," said Parker. "Soon."

So he is going to wait until we get home before he states his intention? thought Berta. *That's really not very sporting of him. What are we to say after being plied with veal cutlets and fresh peach pie?*

But Parker did not even invite himself in when they reached the house. Glenna did. "Aren't you stopping?" she asked sweetly when he seemed to be saying his good-night at the door.

"Not tonight," he answered her. "I'll be by to pick you up for church in the morning."

They all expressed their thanks and moved on into the living room after Parker took his leave.

"What a fine young man," her mother exclaimed as she drew off her gloves.

"Isn't he wonderful?" said Glenna, her eyes full of love. "I am just so—so blessed."

Berta frowned and went to poke in the fireplace. The

flame had gone out, but it was warm enough in the evenings now that they didn't need it. She had no intention of building the fire again. Still she poked. And as she poked she puzzled. What had the evening been all about? Certainly it had been—enjoyable. A special treat for three women who rarely got out. But what had it really been about?

She was still shaking her head in puzzlement as she went to her room to remove her best gown and put on her robe.

Little girl, she mentally addressed her young sister, *you are far more blessed than you even know.*

The question was eventually asked. Parker chose to talk with Mrs. Berdette in private before he took Glenna out for another special dinner. Berta was let in on the secret, but Glenna was totally unsuspecting.

"She thinks it is simply a birthday dinner," Mrs. Berdette confided to Berta, and she beamed at the thought of the pleasure ahead for her younger daughter.

Berta tossed her head. "Surely she's not such a simpleton as that," she exclaimed. "Everyone else in town has smelled it coming for months."

"Glenna is sweetly naive," her mother contended.

Berta let the comment pass.

"So how long is he willing to wait?" she asked her mother.

"Not long, I'm afraid. He wishes to be married in August."

"August! That hardly gives us time to prepare," protested Berta.

"Time enough," said her mother.

"Why is he in such a rush?" demanded Berta.

"He plans to start classes in the fall."

"Classes. For what?"

"You don't know? I thought everyone knew. He's going to be a doctor."

Berta stared, openmouthed. Why hadn't she been told? Even Glenna had said nothing about such plans.

"You didn't know?" asked Mrs. Berdette again.

"No. No, I didn't know," replied Berta. Then added quickly. "Did Glenna?"

Mrs. Berdette looked up quickly, her hand with the needle and trailing thread stilled. "Of course," she replied. "But I think Glenna expected him to finish his training before he considered marriage."

"And why doesn't he?" asked Berta tartly.

"He'll have to go away for the training. They don't teach medicine at our little university here in Allsburg."

"Go away?" Berta didn't like that thought. "Why doesn't he go alone and leave Glenna here—until he's finished?"

Mrs. Berdette let the question go unanswered for a while. At last she spoke. "Glenna is a beautiful girl," she said honestly. "I don't think any man would be comfortable taking a chance on waiting."

"Just because she's—she's pretty doesn't mean she needs to be fickle," replied Berta, her tone sharp.

"Fickle? Glenna?" Mrs. Berdette laughed softly. "Glenna couldn't be fickle if she put her whole mind to it," she said. Then she continued. "I've always been so thankful to God that she didn't get spoiled. With all the attention she has constantly had—she didn't let it go to her head. I used to pray and pray—asking God for wisdom in raising her—asking for her heart to be kept pure—her mind free from conceit."

Her eyes were moist with unshed tears.

"Well, He has answered me," she continued. "Abundantly. I've never met a sweeter, more giving person in my life. Her father would be so proud of his little girl."

Berta stirred uneasily. All the praise for Glenna made her totally uncomfortable. All the things her mother was declaring Glenna to be, Berta knew that she, herself, was not. No wonder her mother had always favored Glenna.

Yes, it was true. Berta had never brought it to the forefront of her mind before. But her mother clearly and unapologetically favored the younger girl.

"How will you ever get along without her?" she asked, letting sarcasm color her words.

Mrs. Berdette looked up. "I won't get along without her," she replied simply. "She'll still be my daughter. I'll just finally be blessed with a son."

"Humph!" snorted Berta. "We'll see," and she rose to her feet and hastily escaped the room.

Chapter Eight

Moving On

The morning of August tenth dawned clear and bright. *Glenna's wedding day* was the first thought that entered Berta's mind as her eyes opened.

"Mama prayed for a beautiful day," said an excited voice from across the room.

Glenna stood at the open window, her long dark hair tumbling about her shoulders, her hand sweeping back the curtain.

"Didn't you?" mumbled Berta in return.

"Oh no," said Glenna, turning slightly. "I wouldn't have dared to—to be so selfish. God has given me so much already."

"Then, I guess you should be thankful for Mama's prayers," Berta retorted and swung her feet over the side of her bed and into the waiting slippers.

Glenna only sighed and let the curtain drop back into place.

"Berta—" she began.

Berta did not look her way. She went to the dressing table that they shared, lifted her brush, and began to stroke the tangles from her long hair.

In the mirror she could see her sister's reflection. She was standing with a bemused look on her pretty face, studying the ring on her finger.

"I am so—blessed," she said at last, but Berta didn't know if she was speaking to her or to herself. "So very blessed. Imagine me—marrying the—the most sought-after young man in town."

Her head swung up, and she clearly began addressing her comments to Berta.

"He is so—so wonderful. Everything about him is so wonderful. I—I feel like—Cinderella."

"Well, Cinderella," said Berta dryly, "if you don't get out of your flannel and into that new dress, you're going to miss the ball."

Glenna giggled. "Oh, Berta," she exclaimed, "I'm going to miss your—your crazy sense of humor."

And Glenna crossed impulsively to her older sister and gave her a warm hug.

It caught Berta totally by surprise. They were not used to sharing intimate moments. There was nothing she could do but return the embrace, and as her arms enclosed the shoulders of the younger girl she suddenly realized that she was going to miss Glenna as well.

Who would be her champion? Who would make her laugh with her bubbling stories of school mishaps? Who would sense her every mood and respond to it with love and understanding?

Berta fought back the tears, then released Glenna and pushed her back from the embrace. "I'm going to put on the coffee," she said in an impatient tone. "You'd best get yourself dressed. We have plenty to do today."

Mrs. Berdette was already in the kitchen. There was much to get done in preparation for the meal that would follow the wedding service. Berta knew it would take all three of them scurrying about all morning to accomplish the tasks.

"Is Glenna awake?" asked her mother.

"Awake—and swooning," replied Berta, not looking her mother's way.

"No wonder," replied Mrs. Berdette, and Berta could tell from the sound of her voice that she was smiling.

"What a lovely couple they make," her mother went on. "She's so beautiful and he's so handsome. They will be so happy."

"I didn't know that one's degree of happiness was determined by how one looks," mumbled Berta as she set the coffeepot to boil.

Mrs. Berdette looked up quickly. "Oh, Berta," she said with a hint of impatience. "I didn't mean that, and you know it."

Berta was silent for a moment as she went for the bread to make toast.

"Still," she said to her mother, "there is truth to it. It was Glenna's—'prettiness' that got her the most prized man in town. And I daresay it was his good looks that drew her attention."

She saw the expression on her mother's face and knew she wished to deny the statement—yet in her honesty could not.

"But it—" began Mrs. Berdette.

"Doesn't seem too fair," continued Berta. "What about us plain people? What chance do we have?"

"You're far from plain, dear," her mother answered.

Berta did not even reply to the remark. She was plain and she knew it. Only a mother would argue against that fact.

Berta was about to speak again when the bride-to-be appeared in a burst of Glenna-energy and a wealth of glowing smiles.

"Mama," she said before she even got through the door, "thank you for your prayers. Look at this glorious day."

Mrs. Berdette put down the pan in her hand and reached out her arms to her younger daughter.

Berta went back to her toast making.

————

Even Berta had to admit it was a beautiful wedding. Glenna was glowing and more lovely than ever, and Berta heard many comments from the gathered crowd concerning that fact. "And so sweet, too," people often as not would add.

"And he's so handsome. They do make a stunning couple, don't they?" the talk went on.

Berta moved away from the voices, her thoughts churning. It didn't seem fair that what happened to one in life was governed by how favored one had been in good looks. Glenna had won Parker. Yet hadn't she, Berta, seen him first? Hadn't he smilingly handed her back her retrieved hankie? But he would have never taken a second look her way, she was sure. She wasn't pretty like Glenna.

She shrugged her shoulders and moved on to check the tables. The food seemed to be evaporating into thin air as the long line of guests moved past to fill their plates.

Without thinking Berta put her hand up to touch her hair, making sure that the tight knob was securely fastened. She was glad she hadn't succumbed and worn it looser and soft about her face. It would be "giving in" to society. Trying to be "pretty" to match its demands. She had no intention of yielding. She would fight the unfair system until the day she died.

Berta had not realized how much she would person-
ally miss Glenna. She had expected her mother to mope.
But Mama seemed reasonably cheerful, as though she
had made up her mind that life must move on and she
didn't intend to let the change get the better of her.

Berta turned her thoughts back to the long-ago conversation. There were more changes ahead. She knew
that. She was sure her mother had not forgotten the idea
of moving in with Granna.

Berta decided that she would make the first move.
She no longer would be at the mercy of others' decisions.

She began to make discreet inquiries in town. There
was very little that she would be able to afford on her
library salary. Well, there was nothing to be done about
it. She would just have to keep inquiring until she found
something inexpensive. Surely there was something—
somewhere.

She was beginning to feel discouraged about the
whole process when Miss Phillips brought word of a Mrs.
Cray who had a room to let. "It's small—but comfy. You
may take your meals with the family, or she'll send them
up to your room," the woman went on.

It sounded wonderful to Berta. She went immediately
to check on it.

Much to her delight the room was well within her
means. She produced the first month's rent on the spot.

"I will be moving in over the weekend," she informed
the lady and hurried back to the library to thank Miss
Phillips for the tip.

Berta's walk home that night was slow and very
thoughtful. She was happy to have taken the initiative
and found a room. Yet she was ashamed of the way she
had gone about it. She should have talked with her

mother first. Should have told her of her intention. Now she would have to walk in and inform her mother that the deed was already done. It hadn't been wise—nor fair.

Berta dreaded the ordeal ahead. Her cheeks flushed at the very thought of her selfish act.

Just to prove I'm in control, she scolded herself. *That's what it's all about. Just to "show" Mama that she doesn't rule my life.* And furthering her guilt came the thought that Glenna would never have done such a thing.

But the reminder of Glenna's considerate ways and the truth of the statement just made Berta's back stiffen.

Well, I'm not Glenna, she huffed. Glenna was never selfish because she did not need to be. She always got whatever she wanted by her good looks alone. And what credit should she get for her good looks? None. She was just born—lucky, that's all.

So Berta's mood was not a yielding one as she entered the door.

She didn't wait to exchange comments with her mother when she was greeted. She hurried to her room and changed the skirt and shirtwaist that she wore as a librarian to those she used for chores in the barn. She would get that work over with as quickly as possible. And, she thought thankfully, she would soon be rid of it altogether. Someone else could have the care of the horses, cows, and chickens.

As she forked hay and tossed out grain, she was reminded that arrangements had not yet been made, that the farm was not yet sold. Well—she didn't care. It wasn't her responsibility. Her mother could see to that. Mama was the one who had made the plans to move in with Granna.

The evening meal began in silence. Mrs. Berdette seemed to sense the dark mood of her daughter and didn't try to force conversation. At last, with grim determination, Berta burst right in with her news. She did not try to ease the blow, did not seek for gentle openings to the subject; she just threw out the bold statement with no advance conversation.

"I'm leaving."

Mrs. Berdette looked up, her eyes registering her surprise.

Berta could only stumble on, trying to get it all over with as quickly as possible.

"Miss Phillips knew a woman with a room to let. I've taken it."

Still Mrs. Berdette did not speak.

"I move in on the weekend," Berta went on.

Her mother's gaze lowered.

"I . . . see," she managed to say quietly.

"Well, you did say you were planning to move in with Granna," Berta flung at her defensively.

"I've been asked . . . yes," replied her mother, still in the same soft tone.

"I'm tired of tending the team—the—the cows and—chickens. I'm worn out by the time I come home at night. It's a long walk into town and—"

"Yes," said her mother, "it's been hard for you."

They again fell into silence.

"This weekend?" her mother asked.

Berta nodded.

"Do you need furnishings?"

"No. It's furnished."

Silence again.

"Will you board as well?"

"She'll send the meals to my room. I preferred that to joining the family."

Her mother nodded and pushed the peas around on her plate with the tine of her fork.

"I'll miss you," she said finally. "You've always been—

my dependable one." She looked up and managed a smile.

Berta choked back tears and the words that she knew would come out all wrong if she spoke them aloud. *Your "dependable" one? Glenna was your beautiful one—your sweet one. I was your dependable one. Is that—some kind of compliment? If so—I fear I miss it. It sounds like an old shoe—a favorite worn-out chair.*

Berta pushed back her plate. "I'm very tired," she managed. "I think I'll go to bed."

Her mother only nodded, but before Berta could turn to go she noticed the tears in her mother's eyes.

———

Things happened very quickly. Within a few days the team had been sold. Uncle John took the two cows to his farm. The chickens were crated up and sent off to market. There were suddenly no chores for Berta to see to when she came home at night.

Her mother gave her time and attention into gathering up household items, like bed linens and towels. She stacked them in Berta's little room on the empty bed that had been Glenna's.

Her solicitude annoyed Berta. With her mother hovering over her, fetching this and presenting that, Berta felt her independence being lost again. The move was no longer "her move" while her mother scurried about helping it to happen smoothly.

"Mama—I do wish you wouldn't fuss," she said in exasperation. "I can look after things myself."

"Of course you can," replied her mother, "but I take pleasure in helping."

"But—" protested Berta.

Her plea to be left on her own seemed to fall on deaf ears.

"When are you going to pack your own things?" Berta asked frankly.

"Don't you worry about me. I have plenty of time. I'll arrange for selling the farm in the spring."

"In the spring? What will you do over the winter?"

"I'll stay here."

"But you can't—"

"Nonsense. I've been on my own before, you know."

"But, Mama—"

"Now don't you go worrying about me. I want a little time. I don't like to rush into things. I will have all winter to think about what I wish to keep and what I'll sell. It will be good for me to have the time. I'm so thankful that I won't have the stock to worry about. We should have done something about them long ago. Saved you all that work and trouble. I don't know why I put it off so—but you know that I've always had a dreadful time making up my mind. Your papa was the decision maker."

Berta did not like the way things were left—but it seemed that the die had been cast.

Chapter Nine

A New Home

"Mrs. Cray is a good cook," Berta remarked to Miss Phillips as the two of them replaced books on shelves at the closing of another day at the library.

Miss Phillips looked up and pushed her small round glasses farther up her straight nose. She made no reply, and Berta wondered for a moment if she had heard and understood her comment.

"She's a good cook," Berta repeated. "She sends me up a fine plate each evening."

Miss Phillips nodded.

"I don't eat much breakfast," Berta added. "I have asked her for just toast and jam. She continues to argue that I should have a nice bowl of porridge, but I—"

Berta stopped. She was rattling on in a most unusual way. She and Miss Phillips rarely said more to each other than "Good-morning" and "Good-night." Berta felt embarrassment coloring her cheeks. She turned slightly away from the older woman to indicate that she had no intention of boring her with further comments.

To Berta's surprise the woman continued the conversation. "That's good. It would be so nice to sit down to a full dinner. I—I'm afraid I'm not much of a cook. When I get home I just take my book and—" She stopped.

Berta found herself taking a closer look at Miss Phillips. She was dreadfully thin and frail. Berta wondered if she ever cooked for herself at all. What did she eat?

"I never did like cooking," the other woman continued firmly as she smacked a heavy tome into place as though that settled that.

She turned and made her way back to her desk by the entrance, where she began to gather her belongings for departure.

Berta continued to study her.

How old is she? she asked herself. *She seems ancient—yet she can't be that old. Older than Mama? Younger. She's not very gray—but she is hollow cheeked and pale. Very frail looking. Tired? Or just bored with life?*

Berta had never seen her on the streets of town. She knew the woman carried home library books to read each evening. And she often exchanged the book the next day. Berta had never thought to wonder how she could read so many books so quickly. Was that all she ever did? Didn't she socialize—even a little? Didn't she have friends? Household chores? Did she even feed herself properly?

No. No, she supposed not. It seemed that Miss Phillips stayed to herself—in her boarding room. Apparently the only appetite she fed was the appetite for reading. One could starve—physically and socially, living in such a way.

Is that what I will become? wondered Berta uneasily as she turned back to the last few books to shelve. *Is that the road I'm taking? I have been holed up in Mrs. Cray's little bedroom, reading my life away ever since I moved into town. Why, I even skipped church last Sunday.*

Berta felt her cheeks warming.

I haven't even been to see Mama. I've still—still been too—annoyed? Proud? I don't know—but I've surely been trying to prove a point. I guess I wanted her to—miss me. To realize how much she'd lost. Not just in Glenna—but in me.

Rarely was Berta so totally honest with herself. Her frankness, even in thought, surprised her now.

So what have I gained? she asked herself. *I've shut myself away in my room with my wonderful books and pretended that I didn't need anything else. Well, maybe I don't—much. But I refuse to become like Miss Phillips— old—and cold—long before my time.*

Was that why Berta had tried to start a conversation with the reluctant Miss Phillips? Had she been missing human contact? And if she didn't make a point of getting out, would she soon be satisfied to just stay in? Always?

Berta slipped the final book into place and turned just as Miss Phillips was pulling on her gloves.

"Good-night, Miss Berdette," the woman said as she gathered up her book for the evening. "I'll see you in the morning. Be sure to lock the door."

Her words rankled Berta.

"I am sure to lock the door every night, Miss Phillips," she replied curtly.

For a moment Miss Phillips looked surprised, then she nodded, turned, and left the small building.

Berta went to gather her own things. "You'd think I was a child," she said aloud.

Berta cast one more glance about the room to make sure everything was in its rightful place, pulled on her light coat, and picked up her gloves and book.

For a moment she stood looking down at the new publication that she held. She was anxious to read it. Already Miss Phillips had perused the book and had returned with a look of satisfaction on her pale face.

With a quick movement before she could change her mind, Berta crossed to the fiction shelves and placed the book firmly into its designated spot. Then she turned away, stepped lively to the door, secured the lock, and pulled the door tightly closed.

There's plenty of daylight left, she mused to herself. *I'll just stop off at Mrs. Cray's, change into some walking shoes, and tell her I'll not be needing a supper tonight, then walk out to see Mama.*

With her resolve in place, Berta began to walk briskly.

———————

The walk to the little farmstead on the edge of town was pleasant. Berta was surprised at how much she had missed walking.

I must get out and walk more, she scolded herself. *I'll be turning into a pumpkin,* she noted as she turned into the lane.

With a face flushed from the exercise and the slight breeze that tugged at her coat sleeves and toyed fruitlessly with her well-secured dark hair, she made her way past the little barn and on toward the house.

She missed the animals. The pair of sleek horses that had always stretched their long necks over the rails and greeted her with a whinny. The round, brown cows that placidly stood in the shade of the barn, mouths languidly working their cud. She even missed the chickens—their shed seemed strangely silent—empty—void of the squawking, clucking occupants.

Glenna was right, thought Berta. *Our lives have changed. So much. Forever.*

She shivered in the warmth of the afternoon.

She wondered if she should knock. After all, this was no longer her home. Yet to knock would have been to acknowledge further change. A painful change. She desperately needed to feel at home here. She needed to feel a part of this place.

She finally opened the door and stepped silently inside, letting her eyes travel over all the familiar things. Tears formed—unbidden. She wiped at them with impatience and straightened her back.

She could hear stirring in the kitchen. She knew her mother must be getting her evening meal. She did hope that the woman was still cooking properly. Was not eating store-bought crackers and calling it a supper, as Miss Phillips was likely doing at that hour.

She moved toward the sound and remembered that it would be wise to give her mother a bit of warning rather than startling her with a sudden appearance.

"Mama," she called just before she stood in the doorway. "Mama—it's Berta."

Mrs. Berdette's head came up and her eyes filled with pleasure. "Berta!"

Just the one word, but it spoke volumes. Berta's eyes threatened to spill over again. She looked down and began to remove her gloves to cover up her intense feelings.

"I thought I should check on you—" she began quickly. She did not wish her mother to know that she herself needed the contact. Needed to come home.

There was no immediate reply, and when Berta lifted her head again to check out the silence she saw her mother brushing unashamedly at her eyes.

"I'm so glad you came," she finally stated simply, and there was no apology for her emotion. "I've missed you."

Berta turned to lay her coat over a kitchen chair.

"How've you been?" asked her mother, crossing over to place a hand on Berta's cheek much like she had done when the girls were still children.

"Fine," said Berta with too much force. "Just fine. And you?"

Her mother smiled. "Fine," she said slowly—deliberately. "Lonesome—but fine."

"You're still here," said Berta, moving toward the cupboards to give a hand with the evening meal. With relief she noted that her mother was indeed cooking—was preparing herself a decent supper.

"Granna's a bit better," replied her mother, as though to say that as long as she wasn't really needed she would put off the move—would stay right where she was, where she was at home.

"Good," said Berta. For one moment she thought about moving back home with her mother. But she just as quickly divorced the thought. That would be an admission of need. Giving in. Folks would think that she couldn't live independently.

They worked in silence, dishing up the vegetables and meat.

"It looks like you were expecting company," Berta commented.

Mrs. Berdette shook her head. "I just can't seem to catch on to cooking for one," she said, and there was wistfulness in her voice.

Then she brightened and added as she wiped her hands on her apron. "Well—tonight I'm glad of it. I won't need to apologize for not having enough."

"No," said Berta as she set a heaping bowl of fluffy mashed potatoes on the table, "you won't need to apologize."

———

"I had another letter from Glenna."

They had taken a second cup of coffee into the living room and were seated in front of the familiar fireplace. Berta had started the fire, though the night was not cool enough to really need its warmth. Still, the crackling flames were comforting, and it felt good just to sit together in companionship.

"How is she?" asked Berta, suddenly reminded that she had not yet answered Glenna's last letter to her. She had wanted her sister to have to wait for her reply—to miss her a bit more. Berta flushed slightly at the thought and stirred restlessly.

"She misses us," her mother was saying, "but she is full of praise and love for Parker. They have found a little church, and she has thrown herself into helping with the children's work—to help her lonely hours, she says."

"That's nice," spoke Berta, too matter-of-factly.

"She has also met a young woman—the wife of another medical student—and they have formed a friendship. That has helped."

Berta nodded. At least Glenna had someone to talk to. Not a Miss Phillips who usually rebuffed every human approach.

"They have a very small apartment—so she doesn't have many household chores," Mrs. Berdette went on.

Berta looked down at her hands. They were clasped too firmly in the folds of her gray flannel skirt. Why was she feeling knotted inside—the way her tense hands appeared to be? Her mother seemed fine—almost at ease with her new situation. The reports on Glenna were—good. Was Berta the only one struggling with this—this drastic change that had affected the lives of each of them? And if so—why? Didn't family matter to the others? Could they just pretend that—?

No. No, of course not. She was the one who had always held herself aloof—even from family closeness.

They—her mother and Glenna—had always been the expressive ones. The ones who made a big issue of the family bonds. The ties.

Then how was it that the two of them seemed to be moving on with their lives while she stayed static? Knotted? Had she needed them far more than she had ever admitted?

Of course not. She—she was moving on—adjusting—just as well—maybe better—than any of them. It was just that she had—lost so much more. Her mother still had the house. Familiar things. She hadn't had to move out yet. To sort through all of those memories that were stored in closets, the attic. Things that belonged to her father, that brought back pain—and joy.

No, her mother's life hadn't really changed that much—yet.

And Glenna—Glenna had her darling Parker. She hadn't lost—she'd gained. Why should Glenna be sorrowing over lost home—lost family?

Berta moved restlessly again. She was the only one who had really been hurt by the change. The only one who had been made to suffer. It frustrated her. It angered her. It wasn't fair. It just wasn't fair at all.

A dark, deep bitterness began to seep into Berta's soul. She did not voice her feelings. Did not even dare to put them into actual thoughts. But they were there. Quiet, intrusive, and affecting her whole being.

She had come to the farm because she had needed to find a bit of what she had lost. To escape the fate of what she might become. But she had not found the peace she had longed for. Had not found her familiar and comfortable niche. She was strangely afloat. On her own. Trying to find a new place in a heartless world. She didn't like the feeling. Didn't welcome it at all.

"I think I should be going," she said, standing suddenly and placing her empty cup on the side table in one quick motion.

"Oh, but you just got here," her mother protested just as quickly.

"I need to go," argued Berta curtly.

"I thought you might stay—the night."

Berta looked at her in surprise. The thought had not entered her mind, but once presented she was surprised at just how much she longed to do so.

"I brought nothing," she managed at last, fighting off the desire to return to her familiar room.

"Do you have plans?"

The innocent question angered Berta even more, though she could not have explained why. Perhaps she felt that she was being questioned, threatening her independence. Perhaps she knew that the true answer would reveal just how empty—how lonely—her life really was. For whatever reason, the simple query disturbed her and made her answer in a way that she later regretted.

"Mama—I am no longer a child. I should be able to come and go as—as I wish."

"Of course, dear," replied her mother. She sounded a bit hurt and sad. Berta regretted her sharp retort, but she did not apologize.

"It gets dark quickly," she said instead. "I do not wish to be tripping my way back to town."

She bent to gather cups and saucers to return them to the kitchen.

"Just leave them," her mother said. "I need something to do with my time."

Berta heard the painful emptiness, the wistfulness in the words. She stopped—cups in hand.

"Why haven't you moved?" she asked sharply.

Her mother sighed deeply and picked absently at her skirts.

"It's hard," she said at last, lifting her eyes to Berta's. "I . . . I dread it. So much . . . so much change . . . so quickly. I miss your father."

Her gaze dropped again and she toyed restlessly with a lace hankie.

"I miss you girls," she continued as she lifted her face again.

Berta saw the tears. They made little wet trails down her soft cheeks and spread to moisten the creases by her mother's mouth.

Berta didn't know what to say.

Her mother finally spoke again, though her voice trembled.

"I know that I must—must prepare myself. Uncle John has found a buyer for the—our little place."

Berta stared openmouthed. What right did Uncle John have to sell their little farm?

"I know it only makes sense. John has worked hard to find us the right buyer. He—he has a developer who wants our land. The city is growing—pushing out its boundaries. This man—buyer—will give us a nice price. More than I would have ever dreamed of. I—I thought we'd be able to share the money. If you—and Glenna wish your—own home, then you can—can afford to—"

But Berta stopped her.

"What are you saying?"

"Uncle John has a buyer."

"I heard that. I mean, you don't need to sell just because Uncle John—"

"I know, Berta," cut in her mother, "but it does make sense. I can't stay on here alone anyway and you and Glenna—"

"I'll come back if I have to."

"No. No I wouldn't want you to do that. Wouldn't want to impose. You have your own life . . ."

If she only knew what a shallow life that is, thought Berta, but she did not voice her words.

"But I wouldn't—" began Berta instead.

"No, I wouldn't ask that of you," her mother argued again. "You need your freedom to make your own decisions. You have cared for me long enough."

"But—"

"Granna needs me anyway. I've put it off too long already."

"But what about you—your needs?"

Her mother looked surprised. As though she hadn't really stopped to consider her own needs. As though she had forgotten how to think of herself after so many years of thinking of the needs of others.

Then she smiled softly.

"My needs will more than be met," she said at last. "The farm land will bring a good price. I will even have money to go visit Glenna."

The words hit Berta like a hard fist. Her mother was grieving for Glenna. She was willing to trade the farm for a visit to her younger daughter.

Berta straightened and went on to the kitchen. The teacups and saucers were set down on the hardness of the wooden countertop with a clatter.

If that's the way it is, then, so be it, she reasoned inwardly. *Why should I grieve over what will never be again if Glenna and Mama can just sail merrily on?*

Berta grabbed her wraps from the kitchen chair and hastily put them on. She was tempted to just leave by the kitchen door, but good sense prevailed and she did go back through the living room to place a cool kiss on her mother's cheek and bid her a reasonably civil good-night.

Chapter Ten

Adjusting

It was a long, thoughtful walk back to town and her small boardinghouse room. Berta tried to sort through her troubled thoughts. She *couldn't* go back, could she? She found herself with a strong inner longing to do so. *It would be all right,* she argued further with herself, *for Mama and I to just stay on at the farm.*

And then she remembered her mother's information that the farm was to be sold. Uncle John, bless him, without even an advanced warning or discussion with her, had convinced her mother that the thing to do was to sell the farm. To a developer. *A developer of what?* she wondered. Why should their father's little "hobby" farm be sold off to some stranger? It was his pride—their home.

For a moment Berta felt a flash of responsibility for this turn of events. If she hadn't been in such a hurry to be off on her own—to prove her independence—then this might not have happened. Well, there was no going back. But she did wish her uncle John had just kept his nose out of family business.

Berta's steps had quickened with her agitation. She purposely made herself slow down again. She needed time to think. Time to work things through while she could still get a breath of fresh air. The closeness of the little boardinghouse room did not lend itself to clear analysis.

She suddenly felt impatience with her small room. She didn't like it. Didn't like it at all. At times she felt she would suffocate there—all shut up by herself with the four close walls, dull wallpaper, and heavy curtains. Even her books could not give her the space she needed.

A house? Of her own? Yes, that was what Mama had said. The farm price was to be divided. If she wished her own house then—it was an enticing thought. Yes. Yes, she would like her own house. A small cottage—somewhere along a nicely treed street. With a yard—and a spot for roses. A walk. Perhaps bird feeders. A kitchen of her own where she could prepare her own meals. Her own cozy fireplace with a crackling log.

Her step quickened again, but this time she did not check her pace. Her little room no longer filled her with the previous sense of confinement. *How long?* she wondered. How long until the farm would be sold and she would be free to be on her own?

Surely with the sale would also come a great sense of release. She would be able to settle in and find peace with life at last.

Berta was feeling anticipation and hope. She now wished that the farm sale would take place quickly. She wondered if she should lend her urgings to those of Uncle John.

I do hope that Mama doesn't dawdle, she found herself fretting. She might delay until the buyer chooses land elsewhere. The thought worried Berta.

But no, her mother was anxious for the sale as well. She wanted to go visit Glenna.

That thought did not please Berta—but at least it

might serve her purpose, she reasoned. With her mother longing to see her younger child, the farm was bound to get sold.

In spite of herself, Berta smiled. Her step quickened. As she continued on down the street she found herself looking at the houses along the way with new interest. Which one would she like to own? What would she look for? A single bedroom? No, perhaps two. Her mama might wish to visit. . . .

The night was softly gathering in about her. Streetlights lent their glow to guide her steps. Muted lamplight spilled out from windows. Wispy smoke curled upward from lit fireplaces. An occasional fragment of conversation carried out to the street. All of these things spoke to Berta of home. A home. It would be so nice to have a home again. A real home. That was what she was missing. That was why she felt so disconnected from life. So restless and dissatisfied. Once she had her own home she'd be able to settle in and find her rightful spot in the world. She would feel whole again.

She smiled again to herself in the darkness.

A porch swing, she mused. *I've always wanted a porch swing—like at Granna's.*

Yes, she would have a porch swing. That was one thing she would insist upon.

———

It was hard to wait. Mrs. Berdette did not seem to be able to bring herself to actually leave her little home. Berta chafed. Then fall moved into another winter, and Uncle John insisted that his sister not spend the cold gray months alone.

Still she did not accept the offer of the developer. Nor did she have her yard sale and pack up her treasures.

Eventually she took only personal items and allowed herself to be moved in with Granna.

"I'll take care of things in the spring," she assured Berta, but Berta secretly wondered if her mother would ever be able to break her ties to the farm.

The winter was an especially cold one, and Berta found herself feeling more and more confined in her little room. At times she even considered joining the family for meals in the big dining room, but in the end she continued to deny herself that small pleasure. It would be admitting defeat—and need. Berta's pride would not allow her to do that.

Stubbornly she carried on. She wondered if she was becoming more and more like her fellow worker. She arrived in the morning, said her curt "good-day," walked through the hours in silence and solitude, said her "good-evening," and went on home with a book tucked under her arm.

But Berta did make one resolve. She would not become a total hermit. She would at least seek some release from her self-inflicted prison on Sundays. And she would insist on tending to her own physical needs by eating properly and getting some exercise.

Berta assigned herself some blocks to walk even on the nippy days. She made the walks more interesting by studying the houses as she passed briskly by. When winter finally ended—as winters always must—she knew every residential area of the town and had already picked five small houses as "possibilities."

She began to secretly hope that one of those families would decide, for one reason or another, that a move was in their best interest.

Why get anxious? she reprimanded herself. *Mama still hasn't parted with the farm.*

She wondered if she would have to add her voice to

her uncle John's and try to get her mother to make the proper decision.

One afternoon Berta looked up from her desk at the library to find her mother standing mutely before her, looking cautiously around as though she might be escorted away if she dared to open her lips within the hallowed halls.

A flash of fear filled Berta. Her mother had never visited the library before. Was something wrong? But no, she didn't appear to be disturbed.

"Hello, Mama," she said in a soft voice, not just to greet her mother but to indicate that it was all right if they spoke to each other.

Her mother nodded, the feather on her bonnet waving gently. It reminded Berta that it had been a long time since her mother had purchased a new hat. Her father would have been chagrined.

"Come in to the side room," invited Berta, rising and leading the way. Her mother followed wordlessly.

Apart from looking pale and drawn, her mother appeared to be fine. *Perhaps it was just the long, cold winter,* reasoned Berta. *She likely hasn't been out since—*

"How are you, Mama?" she asked as she closed the door behind them and indicated a chair.

Her mother smiled for the first time. "It's good to see you, dear," she answered. "I hardly get to speak to you at church. Your uncle is always in such a hurry to get on home."

Berta nodded. It had been a long time since they had really had a visit.

"How's Granna?" asked Berta. Her grandmother had

not been able to get out to church over the winter
months.

"She's doing quite well," replied her mother. "Her ar-
thritis bothers her. She doesn't dare go out in the cold."

"And Glenna?"

"She is well. Parker is terribly busy, but she keeps occupied with the church and friends."

Berta took the other chair, relief coursing through
her. It was not bad news that brought her mother to
town.

Mrs. Berdette drew off her gloves and played with
them absentmindedly. Berta did not know what to say
next.

"We've just closed the deal on the farm," her mother
said suddenly. "Your uncle John and I just came from the
bank."

Berta could only stare. She had waited all winter for
the news, and now that it had finally happened it caught
her off guard and totally unprepared.

"I need to be out by the middle of the month," her
mother went on. "I guess that means I will need to get
ready for a yard sale."

She stopped for a breath, her eyes on Berta's face.
Berta still did not dare to speak.

"I was wondering if there is anything—furniture
maybe—that you'd like. Anything for your new house?
There's no need for me to be selling it if you can find use
for it."

Berta nodded.

"I was wondering," asked her mother, "if you'd
mind—I know that it's an imposition, but I was wondering if—just for a couple of weeks—if you'd consider coming on home—to help me sort through things. You know
how dreadful I am at making hard decisions. . . ."

Slowly Berta nodded as her mother's voice trailed off.

What a wonderful relief that would be. What a pleasure to be out of the stuffy little room and back out into the crisp country air—the open windows—the space to move about.

"I—I could do that," she said calmly.

"I—don't wish to—"

"No—no, that's fine. I don't mind. Really."

Her mother smiled. "That's such a relief, dear," she said with tears in her eyes and reached out to run her hand down Berta's cheek in her familiar way. "You don't know how I've dreaded facing it alone."

"I don't mind," Berta repeated.

"My dependable one," Mrs. Berdette said softly. "What would I ever do without you?"

Berta could not reply. She felt confused. Choked with emotion.

———

The next weeks passed very quickly. Berta could hardly wait for each day at the library to end so she might get home. It was strange. In some ways it was almost like old times to be back in her own room—back with her mother in the little kitchen—back by the fireside as they sorted through another box of memories.

Yet it was so different. Glenna was missing. Glenna with her silvery laughter—her exuberance—her sparkle. The bedroom seemed so empty—almost lifeless without Glenna. Berta could hardly bear the silence.

And the clutter about them in the little house that had always been so neat and tidy was a constant reminder that things were changing. The sorting and packing was difficult to do—not just for Mrs. Berdette but for Berta, as well.

Berta did make decisions about pieces of furniture

and kitchen items that she would like for her own little home—once her purchase had been made. It would have been so much easier to decide if she knew what her home would be like.

Mrs. Berdette also made decisions—on behalf of Glenna. "She always favored that bureau," she said, or, "That was her favorite chair. Remember how she used to curl up in it?" And, "That is the one thing of her father's that she said she would treasure most."

And so evening by evening and room by room, they went through the house, sorting, saving, agonizing, discarding, until one by one each room was cleared and the day of the approaching sale came closer.

"I don't think I want to be here, dear," said Mrs. Berdette. "Do you mind? I think I'll just have your uncle John take me back to Granna's."

Berta felt that she understood. She nodded in agreement. She really wasn't sure if she wished to be there, either.

"Perhaps Uncle John can store your things until you have picked your house," her mother went on. "I know that I've been unfair asking you to tend to my needs before looking after your own, but I don't know how I ever could have done it alone."

She lifted a hand to Berta's cheek again.

"It's fine," murmured Berta. "I don't mind. Really. I'll find a place soon enough."

But inwardly she was most anxious to get herself settled. She could hardly wait to have a home of her own.

———

Berta felt agitated. The summer was slipping by too quickly. She was having a difficult time finding just the right house. It appeared that none of the homeowners of the five little "possibilities" was interested in moving. Berta felt agitated. And then, just as she felt about ready to give up, a new opportunity presented itself. It was a home that she had walked by on countless occasions and had not even considered before. But when the sign announcing that it was for sale appeared on the front lawn, Berta decided to take a closer look.

It wasn't perfect—but Berta decided that it would do. It didn't have a porch swing. In fact, it didn't even have a porch. But perhaps she could have one built on, she decided.

She set in motion the purchasing of the little place, and when things were finally settled, she had Uncle John bring the furniture items from storage. Then she began her shopping to complete her "nest."

Her mother seemed to take great interest in the purchase and insisted on coming to town to take a look at the new home. Then with renewed vigor, she insisted on becoming involved in curtain sewing and decorating. Berta was surprised at her own lack of resistance. She actually welcomed the assistance. She had so little time before another winter would be upon them, and she did want to have her little place homey by the time the weather shut her in again.

She ordered the porch—and the swing—and the builder promised her that he would have it done before the warm days of autumn left them.

"You'll be swinging on your porch before the leaves turn," he promised. "Able to enjoy the fall colors from right here." He waved his hand to indicate the empty spot where he stood—where the new porch was assigned.

Berta nodded calmly, but inside she felt great excitement. She could hardly wait to get settled in her own place.

So she hired the carpenter, accepted the help of her

mother, and spent her short lunch breaks busily combing
the shops to make her final purchases.

Granna even got involved, sending in jars of home-
made preserves from her pantry shelves to stock cupboards, and store from her garden produce to fill con-
tainers in the cool cellar. Aunt Cee sent a warm
comforter and even Glenna mailed a lace runner for the
buffet that had come from their shared farm home.

Berta felt so much excitement that she could not refrain from sharing it—just a bit.

"I've found a little house," she told Miss Phillips, her
voice well controlled, "so I will be moving from Mrs.
Cray's."

The older woman looked up from the book she was
scanning and pushed her small glasses farther up on her
nose.

"I do so appreciate your help in finding Mrs. Cray's
place. It was just what I needed," Berta went on, as
though that excused her breaking their silence.

Miss Phillips nodded.

Berta shifted to her other foot and picked up another
library book. She was about to move on when Miss Phillips surprised her by asking, "A house?"

"Yes," replied Berta. "A small one—on Cedar Street."

Miss Phillips nodded.

"On your own?" she asked as Berta was about to move
off again.

"Yes," replied Berta as she hesitated for the second
time. "On my own."

Miss Phillips nodded again and pushed further at her
glasses.

"That's nice," she commented and returned her eyes
to her book.

Berta stepped away then.

They did not speak again until Miss Phillips was

drawing on her gloves at the end of the day. Berta was tidying up the check-out desk and making a final assessment of the day's lending.

"It must be nice—to have a whole house," the older woman mused, almost to herself.

Berta nodded. "I am looking forward to it," she said, and in spite of her firm control, her voice trembled with excitement.

The woman turned as though to go. "I envy you," she said simply, then reached to pick up her latest reading material.

Just as she reached the door she turned back one last time. "Don't forget to lock the door," she cautioned, and she left Berta to do as bidden.

Chapter Eleven

The Missing Element

Glenna's letter said things were going well. Parker was wonderful. But she missed her family. Still, she was so happy for Berta. So pleased that she was nicely settled in her own little house. Mama had written that it was so cozy—so convenient to the library. She could hardly wait to see it herself.

Berta read the letter, then reread it. She realized that she would enjoy showing her younger sister through her little domain. She pictured them sitting before the open fire, teacups in hand while she presided as hostess of the home. The picture pleased her. She did wish Parker had not taken Glenna so far away from home.

Berta missed her mother. Even though her visits to the family farm had been few, she still felt an emptiness knowing that her mother was not close enough for her to walk out for a chat if she felt the desire. Her grandmother's farm home was too distant to make it a reasonable walk. And it seemed that her uncle John was too busy to make the trip into town for social visits only. Berta did wish that her mother was nearer at hand. She was even tempted to invite her mother to move in and occupy her guest bedroom, but each time the thought occurred she remembered that her mother was already busy caring for her grandmother.

One day after closing the library—and carefully locking the door—Berta did take a walk back out to their farm site. As she turned into the lane, what met her gaze filled her with dismay. Gone was the little barn—the hen house, the root cellar—even all traces of the country garden and the trees and shrubs her father had carefully planted and diligently tended. Gone was the country home with its curtained windows, its wide porch and welcoming door. The outside clothesline, the backyard playhouse—everything that Berta had known since a small child.

In place of all she had known was scarred earth and empty acres, waiting and ready to receive—something. Berta did not know what the developer envisioned for the space he had prepared. She did not wish to know. What did it matter? He had destroyed so much that was good.

Feeling sick, she turned from the scene and walked quickly away. She would never willingly pass that way again.

———

Berta gladly accepted the invitation to share Christmas with the family at her grandmother's house. It would seem like old times—almost.

Of course Glenna would not be there. It was much too far for Glenna and Parker to travel during the short break he had from his classes.

Uncle John and Aunt Cee would be there. So would the married Ada and her husband Peter who farmed nearby. They would bring with them little Peter, Henry, and baby Mirabelle. Berta still found it hard to believe that her cousin already was the mother of three little ones.

William and his new bride would also be there. Berta did not know Constance well.

Dorcas would be absent. Much to Aunt Cee's regret, her new son-in-law had decided that a move was in the best interest of his family, and he had led Dorcas off to the big city many miles away where he was employed in sales for a furniture store. The move had been hard on Aunt Cee. She did not have the future hope of a return of her youngest, as Mrs. Berdette did of Glenna.

The day turned out to be quite different than Berta had expected. Her grandmother was no longer able to take over the meal preparation. She supervised and gave instructions from her chair by the large kitchen table.

Ada was much too busy with her three little ones to be able to assist the other ladies, and William's new bride still felt uncertain and bashful and held back. Aunt Cee was having some difficulty with a bothersome back—so it turned out that Berta and her mother had to cook most of the dinner and then clean it all up. Berta did not mind, but she was weary by day's end and only too happy to retire early.

As she undressed and slipped into her warm flannel gown, she felt a nagging worry in the back of her mind. Was her mother ill or was she simply showing her age? Was caring for her grandmother too much for the slight woman? Mrs. Berdette seemed devoid of her past energy. Her face had looked so drawn by the end of the tiring day. Was it just normal weariness—or was something else the matter with her mother?

She wondered if she should write Glenna about her concern, and then quickly dismissed the thought. It would only trouble Glenna, and there was nothing the girl could do for the situation. Besides, Berta might be wrong. Her mother might be totally renewed after a good night's sleep. After all, she was tired herself. It had been a long, hard day. It was normal to feel weary.

Berta forced herself to dismiss her worrisome thoughts—but she determined that in her two remaining days at her grandmother's, she would keep a close eye on her mother.

———

Berta discovered that Mrs. Berdette still seemed to be weary even after her night's sleep. Berta had asked her mother about it as they prepared cold turkey sandwiches in the kitchen the next day.

"I'm fine," her mother maintained. "Just a bit tired. Granna has trouble sleeping, and I often need to get up with her in the night."

"To do what?" asked Berta frankly.

Her mother shrugged. "That's the sad thing," she replied with a little shrug of her shoulders. "There isn't much that I can do. Sometimes I make her some herb tea or rub her limbs. Or rearrange her pillows. But there really is not much I can do for her. I feel so sorry for Mama. She does suffer dreadfully."

Berta looked at the rather frail-looking woman before her. She loved her grandmother dearly, but she feared what constant care of the elderly woman was doing to her mother.

She opened her mouth to broach the subject and then changed her mind. Instead she turned their attention to her sister. "I thought you were planning a trip to see Glenna," she said.

Her mother's face brightened. "Oh, I'd love to, if only—"

"Surely Aunt Cee can see to Granna for a short time. They live right in the yard."

Her mother still hesitated.

"I'll speak to Aunt Cee and Uncle John," Berta volunteered. "We'll see what can be arranged."

Mrs. Berdette still did not answer, but her eyes held a look of hope and deep gratitude. She reached out and ran a hand down the cheek of her eldest daughter.

———

Berta was happy to return to the peace and quiet of her own little house. It was so nice to be on her own. To have no one else to demand her attention or trouble her thoughts. But, she had to admit, it was also dreadfully quiet and somewhat empty as well.

She had talked with Uncle John and Aunt Cee, and they shared her concern about her mother. Readily they agreed that a trip to see Glenna would be good for her and give her a chance to get some much-needed rest. They assured Berta that they would take care of Granna.

———

And so arrangements were made and Berta saw her mother off on the eastbound train. Excitement filled Mrs. Berdette's eyes and flushed her pale cheeks as she waved goodbye from the train window.

But with the departure of her mother for the planned two months with Glenna, Berta's world seemed even more empty and forlorn. She hadn't realized what it meant just to know that her mother was close-by. Just to be able to greet her casually on Sunday morning—even if they didn't have time to really chat.

"Maybe Glenna's right," Berta said reluctantly to herself one day. "Maybe it helps to be more involved with the church."

Berta determined to pay a visit to the pastor of the small congregation to find some place of service.

"I have a good deal of time to offer," she informed him when they met. "My evenings are quite free. I have only myself to care for, and as I'm an organized person it really doesn't take me much time to tend to my daily tasks."

Pastor Jenkins smiled and welcomed Berta. He said there was a need for a worker with the children. Berta was glad to be actively involved again. She had taught Sunday school as a teenager and had enjoyed the experience. She hadn't realized how much she had missed the children until she began to work with them again. She diligently prepared for each class, using books from the library for additional background and occasionally bringing an appropriate story to read to the children. Soon she could hardly wait for Sunday morning so she might welcome and be welcomed by newly scrubbed, smiling faces.

One duty led to another and soon Berta's evenings, Sundays, and Saturday afternoons were more than full. She reserved Saturday morning to hastily do the tasks that her home demanded and crowded other small chores into the extra minutes she could find here and there. Soon she was so busy she hardly had time to work everything in—but she liked it that way. At least she wasn't bored. And she wasn't getting lean and pale faced and introverted like Miss Phillips. No one could accuse her of becoming the typical old-maid librarian, stern faced and self-absorbed. Could they?

She wasn't quite sure. She still was totally wrapped up in her own little sphere. Her interests had just shifted a bit. Instead of spending all her time stacking books, she

was now aligning children and ordering their religious
world with a practiced and controlling hand.

It's a good life, she told herself. Rewarding and sat-
isfactory. Most of the time she convinced herself that it
was true.

————————

Dear Berta,
    How can I ever thank you for sending Mama to
me? I knew that I missed her dreadfully, but I didn't
know just how much until I saw her get off that
train.
    I'm afraid the trip tired her. She looks quite
drawn and pale. Parker says he will find her a good
tonic. By the time she returns to you we will have
her feeling great!!!

Berta stopped reading. So it wasn't her imagination.
Her mama was worn out from the care of their grandmother. Berta was thankful she had taken the initiative.
Glad that Uncle John and Aunt Cee had agreed to release her mother from her care giving.

I do hope that Parker finds a good tonic, she mused as
she let her eyes fall back to Glenna's letter.

It was the usual news—of new friends, church activities, and Parker's busyness. Berta scanned the pages
quickly. She had to prepare for an evening of Bible lessons with the seven- and eight-year-olds.

————————

"I have the most exciting news," wrote Glenna several weeks later. "You are going to be an auntie! Parker

and I are so excited. And Mama is thrilled that she will
be a grandmother. . . ."

Berta let her eyes drift from the page. A baby. For
Glenna. It hardly seemed possible—and yet her little sister had now been married for over four years. Even
though Berta had felt Glenna had been much too young
to marry, time had been slipping by. Berta could not now
claim that Glenna was too young to be a mother. Many
girls Glenna's age had more than one child.

"It doesn't seem possible," Berta mused aloud.

With the reminder of Glenna's age, Berta could not
help but think of her own. She would soon be twenty-five.
A veritable old maid.

That didn't seem possible either.

Berta did not like the thought. She tried to shift her
mind from it by going back to Glenna's letter.

"I have a doctor for a husband now. Just imagine that!
Parker is working with an older doctor here in the city.
He wishes to put in two years, and then we will be home.
I can hardly wait. You will be able to spoil your niece—
or nephew."

Berta wasn't sure how much spoiling she would do.
Suddenly she wasn't even sure she wanted Glenna to
come back to town. The thought surprised and embarrassed her.

There was such a contrast between her life and Glenna's. Glenna had it all. Looks and . . . yes, her prettiness
had made life easy for her. Now she had a husband and
happiness, and soon she was going to add a child to her
good fortune. Glenna wouldn't say good fortune. She
thought it smacked too much of chance. Glenna would
carefully say "blessings," attributing everything that
happened for good in her life to God.

*Well, if God was responsible and He loved everyone,
why did He decide to favor some and withhold from oth-*

ers? Berta mused. Why did Glenna get the lion's share?
It wasn't fair.

Suddenly Berta rose and tossed the letter on the
small table beside her chair. Life was so desperately—
uneven. It made her angry. The routine life of busyness—
of work, of church, of housekeeping—that she thought
she had learned to accept, now seemed cold—and lifeless.
Without meaning.

Her frustration drove her to pacing. The little house
that she had so longed to have as her own no longer
seemed cozy, but confining.

She had to get out. Berta grabbed a shawl from the
entry hall and went out into the evening to walk. She let
her agitation drive her at a brisk pace over the side-
walks—street by street.

She was several blocks from home before her steps began to slow.

Look at you, she scolded herself. *Glenna writes you
good news, and you can't even rejoice with her. You should
be writing a letter of excited congratulations, and here
you are walking off your snit.*

Well, it's unfair, she argued back. *Glenna already has
all she needs for happiness.*

And what does one need for happiness? an inner voice
seemed to probe.

The thought nearly brought Berta to a halt. She had
never really thought about it before.

Well, I—I—

She had good health. A job that, for the most part, she
enjoyed. A little home all her own. Meaningful activity
to keep both her mind and body busy. What was it she
was lacking?

A spouse? No. No, she wasn't sure that she even
wanted one. She liked her independence. She liked to be
free to make her own way. Then, if she didn't wish to be

married, why was she inwardly jealous of Glenna for the fact that she was?

Berta could not even untangle her own thinking. She just knew that she felt empty—alone—and she had now made the sorrowful discovery that busyness was not going to fill the void in her life.

Chapter Twelve

Glenna

Mrs. Berdette had returned to her duties with Granna by the time Glenna's "darling baby" arrived, a boy whom they named James Edward after his two grandfathers. In spite of Berta's feelings of resentment toward Glenna, who seemed to have life's smile with regularity, it had been hard at first for her to wait to see the child. But eventually she nearly forgot she had a nephew. Time and distance almost put the little one out of her mind.

She still fretted about her mother and made trips to her grandmother's farm to check on the woman. She even purchased a fine mare and a light buggy so the trips might be made more quickly, more often, and in comfort. She enjoyed the mare and the sense of freedom the animal brought with her, but she had no desire to be responsible for her daily grooming and care. So she boarded the animal at a stable on the edge of town.

Her mother did seem a bit rested and restored to her earlier vitality when she had first returned home from her trip to Glenna's, but she very quickly began to look peaked and strained again. It worried Berta. Yet her mother never complained of being in pain or more tired than she should be.

Berta knew it was a burden for the woman, getting on in years herself, to be caring for the elderly Granna. But she didn't know what could be done about it.

She continued her activities with the children of the little congregation. She had faced the fact that bustling about was no substitute for inner satisfaction and peace, but doing so did help to fill many lonely, restless hours. For that much she was thankful.

Miss Phillips continued her duties at the library, but Berta secretly wondered how much longer the frail woman would be able to work. Berta was sure she was not eating right and was often tempted to talk to the woman about the fact. But Miss Phillips was so distant. So reserved. It was most difficult to speak to her about anything.

Two years slowly moved by, and in spite of Berta's underlying dissatisfaction, her life continued on in the same daily manner. With deadly certainty, each calendar month was pulled from the wall and discarded in her kitchen wastebasket. Nothing seemed to really change from day to day, month to month. Her life seemed to be one dull and uninteresting sequence of little routine events.

And then came the day she flipped a page in her daily reminder and saw the note she had written to herself: "Meet Glenna's train. 2:34."

At least this would be a bit of diversion.

She had already arranged to leave the library early. Uncle John and Aunt Cee had promised to bring her mother in from the farm. Berta had invited them all to her little house for tea after they collected Glenna, Parker, and little James. She wasn't quite sure if her intentions were really to welcome Glenna or if she merely wanted to show off her comfortable home to her sister.

Still struggling with conflicting emotions, she wished Glenna would just stay where she was. She seemed quite content there. Why didn't Parker continue to practice medicine alongside the older doctor with whom he had been working? On the other hand, she felt unexplainable excitement at the thought of seeing Glenna again. Glenna was the one person—besides her parents—who seemed quite willing to accept her as she was. Perhaps even love her. Glenna was, and had always been, her champion. For some strange reason, her sister seemed to look up to her, and even to stand up for her.

Berta could not untangle her feelings about Glenna. Life wasn't fair. Perhaps God wasn't even fair—she hadn't settled that question in her mind. But was any of that really Glenna's fault?

So it was with a strange mixture of thoughts and emotions that Berta surveyed her tea preparations one last time, put on her best black skirt, her new white shirtwaist, and her smart but simple bonnet, picked up her shawl and her gloves, and set out for the train station.

When the train was only ten minutes late, Berta decided it must be some kind of record—it could never be counted on to make the run on time, and folks usually didn't start seriously watching for it until an hour or more beyond schedule.

As they stared down the tracks, Berta noticed that her mother's cheeks were flushed with excitement, her eyes bright. The woman had not yet held her grandson, and Berta knew she could hardly contain her emotions.

The tired locomotive rounded the bend with weary chugs and wafting smoke to make its way into the station. Berta found herself standing with rigid shoulders and straight back. For whatever reason, she felt challenged by Glenna's return.

Was she still trying to compete with the younger woman?

The thought was a strange one. Compete? For what? They now lived in two different worlds. Glenna's life very likely would only rarely touch her own. Oh, certainly there was their mother. But she would be their only common interest. *Mama and Granna,* thought Berta. Even Uncle John and Aunt Cee were seldom around anymore. Their own family had expanded and took most of their time and attention.

So Berta lifted her chin and waited for the train to jerk to a halt.

They were the last passengers to disembark. Glenna and Parker stood in the doorway, both with their arms filled with "things." Berta found herself straining to locate the baby, but she saw none. Her gaze returned to Glenna. The years had been more than kind to her. With maturity she had blossomed. If she had been pretty as a young girl—she was lovely now. Lovely and poised and filled with a look of such *satisfaction.* Her face, now flushed with excitement, was a study in beautiful tranquility.

And then Berta saw a red-capped attendant behind them holding a small boy by the hand.

"Where's the baby?" she heard her mother murmur, and Uncle John responded with a hearty, "Think that wee boy belongs to her?"

Berta heard her mother gasp. "Surely not," she argued.

But Berta knew it was true. They had all been expecting Glenna to return with a baby in arms. But two years had passed. Little James was no longer an infant.

And then the two little groups were intertwining.

What a noisy knot of people they made, each one exclaiming and welcoming the others with hugs and greetings, little James claiming the most. At last they began to sort themselves out, and Berta was able to again extend her invitation and suggest that they make their way to her home. There was not room for everyone in Uncle John's buggy.

"I'll walk," responded Berta. "By the time you gather the luggage and get it loaded, I'll have the teakettle on."

"Oh, could I walk with you?" cried Glenna. "I have been shut up in that slow-moving, cramped train for such a long time. I'd love to stretch my legs. Do you mind, dear?" and she turned to Parker.

And so Berta and Glenna started off through the streets of the town.

"How have you been, Berta? You look marvelous," exclaimed Glenna.

Berta could have "humphed" at the remark. She knew that she did not look marvelous. Glenna looked marvelous. She let Glenna's wild statement pass without comment.

"James must keep you busy," she responded instead.

Glenna gave her a look of teasing exasperation. "Oh, that is the understatement of the century," she breathed, then laughed. "He is such a delight," she hurried on, "but an awful lot of energy. Parker is so good with him. Lets him run off a little of that excess liveliness each evening when he comes home."

"I'm surprised Parker gets evenings at home," Berta put in. "I thought doctors were always on call."

"Well, yes—and no," said Glenna. "They take rotations—take turns."

"Do you expect that to continue here?"

Glenna shook her head. "I've no idea. But I don't suppose so. Parker will be establishing his own practice. He will need to be on call for all his patients. It's bound to be different."

She took a deep breath and looked about as she walked. "Oh, it's so good to be back home. Have things changed much?"

Berta tried to replay the years since Glenna had left their town. Yes, things had changed—yet much had stayed the same.

"I guess the farm will be the biggest change you'd notice," she said slowly.

"They changed it?"

"It's gone."

"Gone?" Glenna's eyes grew wide at the thought. "What did they do?" she asked, her voice tremulous.

"They've torn it all down. Built houses there. I don't even go out past the place anymore."

"I can't imagine. It was a beautiful little house. Why would anyone wish to tear it down?"

"They call it progress," said Berta with an exasperated sigh.

They walked in silence for several moments.

"What do you think about Mama?" asked Glenna suddenly.

Berta looked at her younger sister, worry showing in the deep blue eyes.

"I—I think that . . . she's failing," replied Berta, wanting to be completely honest, yet hating the truth.

Glenna nodded solemnly.

"I had hoped the tonic . . ." She let the words trail off.

"It's too hard for her to care for Granna," put in Berta, "but I don't know what to do about it."

"Is it just Granna's care, or is Mama—?"

"I don't know," said Berta, shaking her head. "But it certainly doesn't help for her to have to miss night after night of sleep."

"Maybe Parker can help Granna," mused Glenna aloud.

Perhaps that was the answer.

As the two sisters approached the little house, Berta felt she had everything well under control. She had spent the evening before preparing everything for her guests except for the very last-minute tasks. But still she hurried into the house, removed her gloves, hat, and shawl, and proceeded on to the kitchen while Glenna moved about exclaiming over this and fingering that. Berta had known how Glenna would respond, and her face flushed with pleasure at Glenna's comments.

But she had to get busy if things were to be ready when the buggy-load of visitors appeared at her door.

Glenna soon came to help her, still expressing her delight with Berta's lovely little home.

They were just setting out the sandwiches and cakes when Berta heard the others arrive. From then on the house was filled with a flurry of activity. Berta quickly settled everyone according to her plan—except for the young James. He seemed to be everywhere at once. Berta had never worked with such a distraction underfoot before. She feared she would be running into the small boy with a tray of hot tea. And she kept an alert eye on his rovings as he surveyed her prized possessions. *Has he been taught to keep hands off?* she wondered. Would Glenna or Parker keep their eye on the boy?

By the time Berta had finished serving, she was exhausted by nervous tension. She could hardly wait for everyone to go home so she could clean up and get things back to her comfortable, tidy, normal ways.

"I hope they never bring that child here again," she muttered when the door finally closed and she was alone.

But as she surveyed her little domain, except for used teacups and plates of leftover sandwiches and cakes, the room's furnishings had not been damaged.

"Well—I guess I was lucky this time," she breathed

with a sigh of relief. Had she been honest, she would have acknowledged that the ambitious little boy had been held well in check.

———————

Parker and Glenna settled in a newer community in the town of Allsburg, and Parker set up his practice. From the start it seemed to flourish. Apart from the fact that he was now so busy that they rarely had family time together, Glenna seemed extremely happy.

Berta was prepared to settle back into her familiar routine—but Glenna seemed equally determined to shake her world up a bit. Berta occasionally felt put out by her intrusions, at the same time hesitantly admitting to herself that they did add some spark to life.

Glenna's new mothering role appeared to be extended to include her sister, and Berta wondered if Glenna thought she needed her help to be happy. She resisted, assuring Glenna in her own way that she was totally in control of her own life and liked it quite as it was. Of course, it wasn't entirely true, but Berta secretly wondered if there was such a thing as total happiness.

But Glenna seemed happy.

She had shared the secret that she was expecting her second child—and even though the energetic Jamie seemed to keep her continually on the run, she said she was excited about the idea of pairing him up with another. Berta could not fully appreciate her attitude, but she accepted it. Glenna herself seemed to have boundless energy. Berta was sure that she would need every ounce of it once she had two youngsters running around.

One Wednesday afternoon Berta was busy filing library cards when Glenna burst in upon her, face glowing, eyes bright. With a nod of her head she motioned Berta toward the small private room that they had used on occasion for personal discussions. Berta soundlessly got up and followed.

"Oh, Berta," exclaimed Glenna when she had shut the door. "I've just met the most perfect man."

Berta stared. *You already have a man,* was her first thought, but Glenna bubbled on.

"Can you come for dinner Sunday? I've invited—"

What was her sister saying? Did she think—? Berta's lips closed firmly in a thin, stubborn line.

Yes, she did. Glenna was about to lend a helping hand to find her a desirable suitor.

With a look of angry dismissal, Berta spun on her heel and left the small room, her plain black skirt swishing against the hard oak floor, anger spilling out with each step she took.

This simply was going too far. Too far. She had no intention of letting Glenna—or anyone—try to match her up with a man. She didn't want a man. Didn't want energetic children rushing about her skirts, demanding her total time and attention.

Berta returned to her file cards, her mind still whirling with angry thoughts.

After some time Glenna appeared, her eyes looking as though she had been crying.

"Berta," she whispered in a quiet voice. "I'm so sorry."

Berta only gave her a cold look and returned to her cards.

Glenna slipped away.

Gradually Berta's anger subsided. It really hadn't been such a terrible thing to do. There was no question that Glenna had been out of line, but she hadn't been malicious. She really hadn't intended—

But Berta found it very difficult to forgive.

It wasn't until she sat before her own fireplace, empty

cup in hand that she let her true feelings come to the surface.

Don't you know that men don't want a plain woman? she cried as though Glenna was in her thoughts listening to her argument. *You were born pretty. You don't know what it is to be—plain.*

Berta had never allowed herself to use a term like "ugly." She didn't want to be thought of as ugly and, in truth, she recognized that she really was not. It would have been an exaggeration—and Berta told herself that she was always honest and straightforward. She prided herself in taking things head on. In facing them. Accepting them. Then she moved on.

But there were feelings concerning Glenna that she had never really understood. Even now, she refused to try to sort them out. They were too deep—too confusing—and perhaps too painful. Berta pushed them aside and went to take her cup and saucer back to the kitchen for washing.

She was exhausted. She would retire early.

Chapter Thirteen

Surprise

Glenna never again brought up the matter of the fine man she had met. Nor did she ever try to set Berta up with any other gentlemen.

Others did.

On more than one occasion Berta was invited to dinner by a kind family of the church and found herself seated at the table beside some eligible bachelor in whom she had no interest and with whom she had no intention of pursuing any type of a relationship.

She always went home disgusted and angry from such engagements. She began making excuses to turn down invitations—not knowing just which ones might turn out to be a matchmaking attempt. This only increased her reputation as withdrawn and unfriendly—but she did not care. She refused to let people interfere in her life.

She thought that now she was beginning to understand Miss Phillips better. Perhaps the older woman had gone through the same routine. No wonder she now stayed close to home in her evenings—with her books. At least she did not have to put on a show of pleasure when presented with some bachelor who had obviously already been rejected by most of the female population—and usually for good reason, thought Berta.

So Berta kept up with her activities. Her busy life kept her occupied and also provided her with an honest reason for not accepting invitations.

But Sundays presented a problem. She could not use the excuse that she had too much to do. Her duties in the Sunday school were over at an early hour. So Berta chose to use her mare for more frequent visits to her grandmother's farm on Sunday afternoons, giving her another reason to be unavailable for those after-church meals. It also gave her opportunity to keep a more watchful eye on her mother and to help her with her duties for at least one day of the week.

Granna was almost totally bedridden now. Uncle John came to do the lifting, but other than that, her mother cared for the elderly woman day by day. Berta knew it was not an easy task. No wonder her mother looked pale and weary.

So Berta took over the duties on Sunday afternoons and suggested that her mother take a rest.

At first Mrs. Berdette had argued mildly, but when Berta insisted, she looked relieved and went off to her room. Berta was surprised at how long she slept each Sunday afternoon. While her mother rested, Berta read. As long as Granna stayed alert, Berta read aloud, but when it was plain that the elderly woman slept, Berta read to herself.

At day's end, Berta prepared a light meal for the three of them, then hitched the mare to the buggy and made the trip back into town.

Often darkness was falling by the time she turned in at the stable and walked the remainder of the way to her little house. She was always weary when the day was over and was glad she didn't need to go through the routine every day.

She could no longer look forward to Sunday as a day of rest and relaxation, though she did look forward to seeing her mother. Because of her grandmother's confinement, Uncle John or Aunt Cee occasionally took turns staying home from services on Sundays so Mrs. Berdette could attend.

Glenna sometimes was able to get out to see her mother during the week. Parker hired a driver to take her and little Jamie to the farm. Glenna was in no condition to do the driving herself, with an energetic son to watch and a new baby on the way.

With their separate lives and schedules, the two sisters were not able to be at Granna's at the same time. Berta did not mind. It was hard enough caring for the two older ladies. It would have been doubly so trying to keep Jamie out from underfoot.

At least that's what Berta constantly told herself. In truth, she had some inner conflicts concerning Jamie. He was rambunctious—tiring to even watch as he dashed about investigating everything in sight. He was also bright and enthusiastic—like his mother—and extremely loving. Each Sunday at church he greeted his "Auntie Berty" with warmth and pleasure, insisting that she bend over for his hug, attended by a kiss on the cheek. Berta pretended to be unaffected, but the truth was she looked forward to his greeting. Never had anyone been so totally and openly pleased to see her.

Berta was secretly afraid that she might be taken in by the small Jamie, so she braced herself and held herself somewhat aloof. But Jamie did not seem to notice. He still headed directly toward her as soon as his papa had deposited him within the safe confines of the church building.

"I wanna sit with Auntie Berty," he would often insist, and Berta's heart would race a bit faster.

"Only if you sit very still," was Glenna's usual reply.

"I will. I promise," Jamie would plead his case.

Berta insisted that he keep his promise. Whenever he squirmed the least bit she gave him a stern look. She was always sure he would reject her the next Sunday, but he never did.

It was a strange relationship, with the little boy offering so much love and Berta working hard to keep it from penetrating her self-constructed shell.

One fall Sunday Berta found herself alone in the foyer when Jamie came bounding in for morning class. As usual his eyes shone as he called out to her and rushed directly toward her.

She felt her back stiffen. This nephew was going to turn her into sentimental mush if she didn't keep up her guard.

But she did bend down for his welcoming hug. She could not totally rebuff a child—could she?

With arms wrapped about her neck he placed a rather wet kiss on her cheek, then leaned back to grin at her.

Berta could not refrain from returning the smile.

"What a lovely picture," said a male voice beside her. Someone else had entered the hall.

Berta untangled Jamie's arms, settled her face into its usual stoic look, and rose to her full height.

A tall man, looking strangely familiar, stood before her. A frown creased her forehead.

"Off to your class now, Jamie," she said to the boy and he bounded away.

"Your son?" asked the gentleman, and when he spoke Berta knew at once who he was. Thomas Hawkins. Years before he had left their area. She'd had no idea he had returned.

"Thomas?" she found herself saying, then quickly changed it to, "Mr. Hawkins—I—I had no idea—"

"I much prefer Thomas," he answered easily, and Berta found herself flushing.

"I didn't know—" she began again. She flushed more deeply at the unbidden thought that his trim beard was most becoming.

"Your son?" he asked again.

Berta became flustered and embarrassed that Thomas—that anyone had watched the affectionate exchange.

"No—no, Glenna's. Remember Glenna?"

Of course he would remember Glenna. Any man would remember Glenna.

"She's back?" he asked, his left eyebrow lifting.

"Yes—she and Parker have been back for almost a year now. Parker has a practice in town."

"How nice," he responded.

They stood there—awkwardly, Berta felt. Again her cheeks colored.

"I must get to my class," she said. "Do excuse me."

He smiled. He had a very nice smile, Berta noted. She had never noticed it when they had been schoolmates. But then she had not liked Thomas Hawkins when they had been schoolmates. He had been a noisy, overly energetic boy, who teased her whenever he had the opportunity.

She had not even liked him in her teens when he had grinned at her whenever they met face-to-face and even dared to ask to walk her home.

No, she had not liked Thomas Hawkins. She supposed that he had not changed. She had no intention of liking him now either.

———

Jamie sat with her during church. When she frowned at him for his restlessness, he leaned up against her and soon dropped off to sleep. She had to place her arm around him for proper support. She didn't want him to wake up with a kink in his neck. Or worse yet, turn in his sleep and slip off the pew to the floor.

It was an awkward position, and Berta found her arm aching by the time the pastor had finished his sermon.

But Jamie seemed to waken refreshed and ready to go again.

"Will you come to our house, Auntie Berty?" he pleaded as they made their way to the church door.

"I need to go out to see Grandma and Granna," she answered him.

"Can I go with you?" he asked eagerly.

For one moment Berta was tempted to agree, and then she thought of trying to keep Jamie entertained while her mother rested and Granna needed care. It would be most difficult.

"I'm afraid not," she replied. "I will be very busy."

He did not coax further, but Berta saw the look of disappointment cloud his dark eyes.

They were almost to the door when he turned his face up to hers again. "I could help you," he offered quietly and slipped his small hand into hers.

In spite of herself, her hand tightened on the little one. But again she shook her head.

"Jamie," Glenna called as they reached the outside steps of the church.

Jamie took one more look at his aunt and then released her hand.

"See you next week," he said in grown-up fashion and ran off to his mother.

Berta gathered her teaching materials into a more compact bundle and prepared for her walk home. She would deposit her load, grab a quick bite to eat, and hurry off to the livery to collect her mare and buggy.

With thoughts on her afternoon ahead, she hardly noticed that someone had fallen in step beside her until a voice spoke.

"May I walk along with you?"

Berta looked up to see Thomas Hawkins at her side.

He had not asked if he could see her home. That she would have quickly declined. He had simply asked to walk along with her. It was a public sidewalk. She could hardly refuse that.

"I hear you are the librarian," he said at her prim nod of agreement. "I expect to make much use of the library in the coming days. I thought you might be able to give me some idea of what I can expect to find there."

"In what regard?" asked Berta, not taking her eyes from where she was placing her feet.

"I'll be teaching at the university this term," he went on. "History."

A silence fell. Berta mentally went over their shelves of history.

"We have a fair selection," she said in businesslike fashion. "It will depend on what you are looking for. We might be able to offer material."

"Very good!" He smiled at her and she could not avoid making eye contact. It made her feel uneasy and she found herself stiffening again.

"Doesn't the university have its own library?" she asked rather curtly.

He nodded. "It does. But it's always good to supplement the material as much as possible. The students will also have access to the university material. I like to throw in a few surprises."

He smiled again.

"I didn't know you had pursued your education,"

Berta commented for something to say.

"We haven't been in touch," he answered matter-of-factly. "I didn't know you were a librarian."

She looked at him frankly as though to ask where and how he had learned that information. He seemed to read her thoughts.

"I asked Parker. He said you are doing very well. Have your own place on Cedar."

Berta wondered what else Parker might have passed along. She was a bit miffed at Parker. Yet she had no reason to be. Nothing he had told Thomas so far could be considered private.

"What else did Parker divulge?" she asked dourly.

"That you make a great auntie," Thomas reported with a smile.

Berta cringed. Jamie was turning her into a sentimental old dolt.

"He also said that you are kept on the run—caring for your mother and grandmother each Sunday, teaching Sunday school, working at the church many week-nights—"

"But not every weekend," argued Berta quickly.

"No? He also said that you are involved in some community activities with boys and girls."

Berta did not respond.

"How do you do it?" he asked, his eyes reflecting admiration.

Berta felt her cheeks flushing. She was not used to a gentleman looking at her in such a way.

"I have no one else to—" she began, and then quickly broke off. She had not intended to share that fact with Thomas. He did not look surprised.

"You must have boundless energy," he replied.

"Does it surprise you?" she asked curtly, thinking of Miss Phillips. "Is the librarian image one of a quaint old maid with her nose in a book and her cheeks pale from lack of sun and air?"

Her question was too sharp. Too direct. She wished she could take it back. To her surprise he laughed. A gentle laugh that rolled softly from his lips and made his eyes crinkle with merriment.

"You haven't lost your spark," he replied, looking as though he meant it as a compliment.

Berta was totally discomfited. She did not know how to respond to this boy-turned-man.

They approached her house, and she was glad she was able to turn in at her gate.

He did not rush away but leaned on the fence and looked at the house.

"It's a lovely little place," he mused. "You must take great pleasure in it."

Berta nodded. If he wished her to extend an invitation he was to be disappointed. She had no intention of asking him in.

"Well, I'll see you at the library," he said as he straightened and waved his hand cheerily.

Berta watched him go, her thoughts whirling around in her mind. Why had Thomas Hawkins returned to their little town? And an even more troubling thought, why did she really care?

Chapter Fourteen

The Ride

Thomas stopped by the library the very next day. He asked for help in discovering the history shelves, though Berta was sure he could have found them well enough on his own.

He spent the morning browsing among the books. He even took notes, convincing a rather skeptical Berta that he was serious about his research.

He was back again the next day. Referring to his notes, he asked Berta if she knew of any fictional work set at the time of the French Revolution. Berta looked up what they had on the subject and found three books for him.

"Sometimes one can glean a good deal from fiction," was his comment. "It is often easier to get a feel of the time in that manner than in reading the history texts," he added as he gathered up the volumes Berta had located for him. She nodded her agreement.

Berta glanced his way now and then and found him totally absorbed in his reading.

He checked one book out and took it with him. "Most interesting," he mused. "Have you read it?"

Berta shook her head. She had noted the book when it came in, but it looked like heavy reading. Berta liked to relax when she sat down with a book in the evenings.

"You must," he urged her. "I'm sure you'd enjoy it."

"Perhaps I'm not as interested in the French Revolution as you are," she countered without looking up to meet his gaze.

He chuckled. "Perhaps not," he conceded. "Though my initial interest was driven by necessity. Now, however, I can't get enough of the topic. It is most fascinating."

Berta did look up then. "Fascinating? Violent and bloodthirsty, you mean," she countered.

"Yes, I suppose it was. But no worse than many other times in our world's history—most recently in Europe."

Berta shook her head. "It's appalling that mankind never learns," she responded. "We still treat one another in ways most inhuman. God must weep as He watches."

His face turned serious to match her mood.

"I'm sure He does," he replied.

They stood in silence for a moment. Berta was the first to speak.

"So what does one hope to accomplish in teaching history? When we learn of wars, revolutions, inhumanities—does it really improve our thinking? Are those students with their knowledge any better than the generation that preceded them?"

It was spoken as a challenge. He did not seem to take it as such. His answer, rather than refuting her statement, agreed with her position.

"We don't learn in the classroom any better than we learn from direct observation, do we? It's a shame—but it's a truth. As you said, you'd think that after all these years of seeing the pain and suffering—the absolute futility of war—that we would have learned that it is not the answer. But greed and avarice and hunger for power seem to dog each generation. That wasn't what God intended for mankind. As you say, it would seem that God is powerless to change man."

I never said that, Berta could have defended herself. But in a way he had seemed to know what her query had intended. She had never had such a discussion with anyone else, nor had she known anyone to read her so well— anyone who had been interested enough in her thoughts to try.

"Well—I think we both know that God is still powerful—man is the problem. Too wayward to listen. . . ." He paused, then, "But I must go. I have a luncheon meeting and I'll be late if I don't hurry. Thank you so much for all your help."

He smiled again, picked up his book and his hat, and departed.

Berta stood still long after his tall figure disappeared through the door.

———

Berta soon became accustomed to seeing Thomas in the library. He would enter with a warm smile and a nod of greeting and begin his search through the shelves.

Then the fall classes at the university began, and his visits were less frequent. Berta would never have admitted the fact that she missed him, even to herself.

———

When winter arrived again, Berta did not really mind, though it did make the trips to the farm on Sundays more difficult. She did not attempt it if the weather was stormy, since her mother worried about her out alone on the roads.

One Sunday after the church service, Berta gathered her books and prepared for her quick walk home before going for the mare and buggy. She paused on the front steps to look at the sky. The bright sun and light wind meant her buggy ride would be comfortable.

"Not a bad day," Thomas observed, falling into stride beside her as he often did.

"Rather nice," answered Berta.

"You'll be going to the farm?"

"Yes—I'm planning to. I didn't make it out last Sunday. The wind was too cold."

"Do you mind if I tag along?"

Before Berta could even answer he continued, "I haven't seen your grandmother for years. Nor have I had the chance to drive by our old farm. Still have a bit of a soft spot for it. Like to see if it looks the same. If you don't mind. . . ." His words trailed off as he waited for her answer.

Berta was still mentally sorting out her response to the request. Was he being terribly forward? Yet how could she refuse an old neighbor the offer of a ride?

"If you like," she said at last, "though it may not be that short or pleasant a trip. Mama usually takes a rest when I am there, and Granna sleeps most all the time now."

He nodded. "Then perhaps I can busy myself with chores of some kind. Haul wood. Water."

Berta smiled. "Uncle John does those things—or one of the boys," she answered.

"Well, then," he replied matter-of-factly. "I guess I'll just ride along and view the countryside. Do you mind?"

Berta did wish he hadn't asked her that. She did mind. In a way. But why should she? He was an old school friend. A neighbor. There really was no harm in him tagging along. Yet she did hope he wouldn't presume on the courtesy and make a nuisance of himself.

"It's fine," she responded, her tone carefully expressionless.

She could feel his eyes on her face, but he made no comment.

When they reached her house she wondered if he expected her to ask him in.

"It takes me about half an hour to be ready to go," she said before he could ask. "Do you wish to meet me at the livery stable?"

"I've never been to the livery—not having a horse," he replied. "If it's all right with you I'll just come back here."

Berta nodded.

"In half an hour?" he repeated.

Berta nodded again.

"I'll be here," he said and walked on.

Berta had no idea where he lived or how long it would take him to get home, change, eat, and be back again.

If he's not here, I'll go without him, she said stubbornly to herself as she went into her house.

But he was there. And he had changed. He was wearing a much heavier coat and warm mittens, and a scarf dangled about his neck.

Berta began the walk to the livery.

"It could get nippy before we get back," he commented as he moved along beside her.

"Perhaps you'd rather not go," replied Berta.

"I think I can manage it," he said with a grin.

It was obvious he had no intention of letting her sharp retorts disturb him.

———

The trip was not as unpleasant as Berta anticipated. He was not a constant talker, but he did make occasional comments that she found either amusing or interesting.

"Look at it," he said as they neared his old farm site. "It looks almost the way it did when Pa sold it and moved out."

"Why did he sell?" Berta asked him, surprising even herself with her direct question.

"Mama never did like the farm," he responded. "Couldn't wait to get back to the city. Pa hated the city. It was an impossible situation. I think it meant the early death of Pa." He shrugged. "Of course, how can one ever know if it would have been different had he stayed on the farm? Ma said he worked himself to death trying to make a crop grow. Maybe she's right."

"Your mother is still living?"

"She remarried," he replied, his answer explaining why he felt free to come back to his old home area.

"What's he like?" she asked him. She had at one time feared her own mother might remarry. She was sure she never could have accepted another man in the place of her father.

"He's—nice. A gentleman. Rather—well situated. Mama is nicely taken care of."

"But you don't think of him as a father?" queried Berta, turning slightly so she could look at him.

"A father? No—no, I don't think of him in that way. I was too old, I guess, before it happened. I had already gone to the university. I never did live with them."

"Did you mind?" asked Berta frankly.

He did not answer immediately. When he did his words were thoughtful. "I don't suppose one ever welcomes a second marriage for a parent. You know, you sort of see your parents as a team. You just can't picture the one without the other. So—in a way, though I didn't mind—I was happy for my mother—still it wasn't—easy to make the adjustment in my thinking. Silly, isn't it?" and he turned to her.

"I don't think it's silly at all," she responded. "I would have been very angry with my mama if she'd decided to remarry. It would have been like losing Papa all over again."

He thought for a long time. Then he nodded. "Something like that," he agreed and fell into silence again.

He took care of the mare when they reached the farmyard, and Berta hurried into the house to see how her mother and grandmother were faring.

Her mother greeted her warmly.

"I was so hoping you'd come today, dear," she said, inviting Berta into the warmth of the fire. "The week seems so long when I don't see you. Glenna wasn't able to come out, either. I don't know how much I will see of her these days. I don't think it's wise for her to travel about now."

"How's Granna?" asked Berta as she removed her heavy coat.

"She's having a better day today. She might even visit with you some."

That was good news to Berta.

"Who's with you?" Mrs. Berdette asked, looking out the window.

"With me?" repeated Berta.

"There's someone caring for your horse," Mrs. Berdette explained.

"Oh—him," acknowledged Berta with a little wave of her hand. "That's Thomas."

"Thomas Hawkins?"

Berta nodded. Mrs. Berdette smiled. "That's nice, dear," she said. "He's a fine young man. I've chatted with him some in church since he returned. He's matured into a fine gentleman. It's nice—"

Now just a minute, thought Berta. *Don't make this into something it is not.* To her mother she said, "He just rode along because he was interested in what had become of their old farm."

The smile left Mrs. Berdette's face.

"And he wanted to visit—you and Granna," Berta hurried on.

"That's nice," Mrs. Berdette said again, and the smile returned.

It was not long until Thomas too was in the house and out of his heavy coat. Mrs. Berdette refused Berta's invitation to take an afternoon nap. Instead she busied herself setting out tea things. Berta left them visiting and went to check on her grandmother.

Granna *was* having a better day. She appeared bright and even requested that her pillows be raised a bit so she might see what was going on.

"Do you wish for me to read to you?" asked Berta after she had her grandmother settled.

"Who's that?" asked her grandmother loudly, her hearing loss making her speak at a higher volume.

"What do you mean?" asked Berta. "I'm Berta—your granddaughter."

"'Course you're Berta," replied the old lady with a snort of disgust. She had become caustic and forthright with aging and illness. Berta often was shocked at the change in her. She had always viewed her grandmother as such a gentle, sweet woman.

"I know my own granddaughter," the elderly woman went on frankly. "Who's that talking? In the kitchen with your mother. That's not John's voice."

"No, it's not Uncle John," replied Berta, surprised that Granna could hear the difference in the voices between the two men. "That's Thomas Hawkins."

"Thomas who?" asked her grandmother, cupping her ear.

Embarrassed, Berta shouted, "That is Thomas Hawkins visiting with Mama, Granna." She was sure he could hear her yelling his name all the way from the kitchen. At least he would know why she was shouting about him, she thought.

"Thomas Hawkins? Do I know him?" asked her grandmother.

"He used to live nearby," replied Berta in a loud voice. "His folks were neighbors."

"You mean that Jedd Hawkins with the uppity wife?" her grandmother yelled back.

Berta felt her face turning crimson. How was she to answer that?

"Would you like your back rubbed, Granna?" Berta hollered in the hope of changing the topic.

But her grandmother was not to be easily diverted.

"This Hawkins fella," she said loudly, "he your beau?"

Berta felt so embarrassed she wanted to run from the room. "No, Granna," she responded as quickly as she could. "He is a friend of the family. He wished to visit Mama."

"Sounds mighty fishy to me," said the old woman with a knowing snort. "Your mama is beyond the courting stage. Why a fella be wanting to visit her?"

Before Berta could answer, her grandmother continued, "Wondered if you'd give my back a bit of a rub. Got a spot of misery right by that left shoulder."

Berta at once obliged.

Chapter Fifteen

Questions

"Do you have plans for tonight?"

Berta's head came up from the list of books that she was checking and looked into the gray eyes of Thomas.

Her mind did not grasp his simple words. She shook her head to clear it and muttered, "Sorry. I—I'm afraid I don't understand."

He smiled.

"I was wondering if you have made plans for tonight," he repeated.

Why were her plans of any concern to him? She just looked at him blankly.

"I thought if you are free we might have dinner," he explained slowly.

Berta finally understood the full import of the question. Her face began to flush, but not with embarrassment. She was angry. Angry that Thomas had presumed she would wish to dine with him just because she had allowed a small friendship.

Or was it even a friendship?

Certainly in her thinking it was not a special friendship. He was an old schoolmate. A member of an old neighbor family. He was a library patron. A part of their town.

And that was all.

Berta wanted no association other than that. Why did Thomas wish to take advantage of the tenuous relationship? Why push for more than she had any intention of giving?

She stood to her full height. Even at her five feet five, Thomas seemed to tower above her, but she lifted her chin and looked directly into his eyes.

"Actually," she said precisely, "I do have plans for tonight. But if I did not—I still would not accept your invitation. I have no intention—none whatever—of forming any kind of—attachment—to any man."

Her eyes held his. She saw the confusion, then disappointment, that darkened his.

"I see," he said at length. He nodded slightly.

Berta still did not drop her gaze, though it was most difficult for her to see the hurt in his face.

"I—I am sorry for assuming more than I had a right to," he said with measured politeness. "Though to be perfectly honest—since we have chosen to be direct—I did not really think of having dinner together as becoming—attached."

Berta dropped her gaze as her cheeks again flushed. She had read far too much into the simple invitation.

"However, to be further honest," he paused for a moment and then went on, "I must admit that I did hope our relationship would extend beyond tonight's dinner invitation."

Berta looked up again. She could see the plea for understanding in the gaze he turned on her. She could say nothing. She was thankful there were no other browsers in the library. Even Miss Phillips had gone home early.

"Are you saying that is an impossibility?" he finally asked her directly.

"I can't imagine why—why you'd even—desire it," Berta stammered, one hand smoothing imaginary wrinkles from her well-pressed gray skirt.

He looked surprised. Then he smiled softly and shook his head. "You mean you didn't understand all my teasing when we were kids?"

"No. No, I didn't understand the teasing. I thought you were a—a rude, impudent boy," she went on honestly, her chin lifting again.

He laughed outright. A very merry laugh. Filled with good humor. It was difficult for Berta to maintain her cool aloofness.

"I suppose you never understood why I hung around in high school—hoping you'd drop something so I'd be the one to pick it up."

He chuckled again.

Berta drew in her breath. "Surely you're not serious?" she managed to ask.

His face turned sober. "Oh, I'm serious all right," he replied.

Their eyes locked again and held for a moment. Berta was the first to look down. She fidgeted nervously with a pencil on the desk. She had never felt so uncomfortable in her life. She wished he would just pick up his pile of books and leave.

"I've always cared for you, Berta," he said softly. "I— don't suppose that is ever going to change."

Silence again.

"Berta, are you telling me that you would never be able to—feel anything for me? Would not even be willing to—to explore the possibilities?" he asked softly.

She shook her head slowly. Her head was whirling with confusing thoughts. She had never considered that

a man—any man—might think of her—in that way.
Glenna, the pretty one, was the one who had always had
the boys swooning at her feet. It was Glenna who brought
the foolish smiles, the scrambling for favored position,
and the daring deeds for even a bit of her attention.

"I—I'm sorry," replied Berta. "I had never considered
. . . No. No, I'm afraid that isn't possible," she finished in
a whisper.

With each word her resolve deepened. She had never
thought of being courted. She had never considered re-
sponding to courtship, to marriage. She was settled. Independent. Her mother needed her. There was simply no
reason for her to even think of changing her pattern of
life. She liked it. Liked being on her own. Liked being
able to make her own plans. To come and go as she
pleased. And what if she allowed Thomas to call and then
it didn't work out? What if he discovered that she wasn't
at all what he wanted—in a wife? What if he—?

"No," she shook her head again and moved back a
step, even though there was a large wooden desk between them.

"I see."

His voice was low. So soft that Berta had to strain to
hear the words.

He began to pick up the little stack of books he had
placed on her desk.

"I will not pretend," he continued. "I am terribly disappointed. I had hoped that—you would feel differently. . . ." He reached for his hat.

"No," said Berta again and shook her head once more.

She heard him sigh deeply, but she did not lift her
head to look into the gray eyes.

She wished he would go. His presence unnerved her.

"Friends, then?" he asked, his voice back to normal.

Berta looked up. She felt confused. She didn't even

wish his friendship, but how could one refuse to be a friend? He lived in her town and attended her church. She could not declare war.

"Yes, of—of course," she managed with a little nod.

He smiled.

"Good," he replied. "Open, honest, direct friends. Okay? If you feel—uncomfortable—like you feel now—" He stopped and smiled. She was surprised that he knew how she was feeling. "Then you say so," he went on. "Tell me exactly what you are thinking—feeling—as a friend."

Berta raised her head. "Are you suggesting—sharing secrets?" she asked forthrightly.

He smiled at that.

"I don't suppose either one of us has many secrets to tell," he observed candidly. "We are both too open and direct with our lives."

"Then—" Berta did not finish the question. She knew he would understand what she was asking.

"If we are going to be friends—without interfering in each other's lives—if we are going to keep the—boundaries that are desired—without making the other uncomfortable—then we must be honest with each other. Right?"

He waited for her to nod or answer. She did not.

"I couldn't do that," she finally said.

"What do you mean, you couldn't?"

"I've never done that—with anyone. I've never shared how I feel. I just couldn't do that."

"We must—"

"Wait a minute," Berta said, lifting a hand to stop him. She sat down in her desk chair and looked up at him, challenge in her eyes. "How come you're making all the rules?" she asked directly.

"Somebody has to make the rules."

"Well—why should it be you? I mean—a friendship is

to be mutual—a sharing—and you're—" She felt so agitated that she stood to her feet again.

"So you feel challenged?"

"Challenged? Ordered. You're telling me what I have to do to be your friend."

"And?"

"And I don't like it. I managed fine without your—friendship, I can go right on managing fine without it. I don't need—"

"Good," he interrupted, and he smiled.

"Good?"

"You've got it. Honest and direct. You just told me exactly what you thought and felt. We won't even have to practice." He smiled again.

For a moment Berta's temper flared. She was so angry that he had—had manipulated things, had set her up. He had just proved to her that she was more than capable of sharing her feelings directly.

Then she saw the humor in the situation and gradually her anger began to seep away.

"I—I guess I can," she said in admission. She even managed the hint of a smile.

He chuckled. Then sobered.

"An honesty without barbs or malice. Taken without offense or pique," he said quietly.

She nodded. "I guess I can do that," she began, then quickly added, "as long as it's not an invasion of privacy. A person has a right to private thoughts and feelings."

"Of course," he answered, a twinkle in his eye. "I don't intend to talk about every thought of mine with you either."

She nodded and began to tidy the things on her desk. It was already past library hours.

He tucked the books more securely under his arm.

"Are you finished for the day?" he asked her.

She nodded as she glanced at the wall clock. "My word! I'll be late for Children's Club if I don't hurry," she said and hastened to get her hat and gloves.

He held the door while she passed through it and turned back to him.

"Make sure it's locked," she instructed in a wry tone, "or Miss Phillips will have my head."

He chuckled softly as he pulled the door firmly shut and tried the handle.

"Locked," he replied.

He fell into step beside her, and she didn't even notice. She didn't notice his smile either.

"What did you think of the service?"

Thomas posed the question as they walked home from church together.

Berta looked up in surprise. "What do you mean?" she asked, a frown furrowing her brow. She had never thought to have an opinion about the service. Services just happened. One attended them and accepted them— one did not *think* about them.

"I'm wondering if Pastor Jenkins isn't getting a little—what should I say?—road-weary," he replied.

"Road-weary?"

He nodded.

"That's a bit—harsh, isn't it?" contended Berta.

"Is it?"

They walked in silence.

"Or is it just being honest?" he asked again.

Berta turned to him. "Being honest again, are we?" she chided knowingly.

"I thought that's what we had agreed to be. Without—"

"Barbs or malice," finished Berta.

He chuckled.

They continued down the wooden sidewalk, both busy with their own thoughts.

"I don't know," Berta at last responded. "Perhaps he is tired. He's been at it for a long time. He was the pastor when I was a child."

Seeing the twinkle in his eyes, she quickly went on, "And not one comment from you."

He laughed softly.

Berta was not sensitive about the fact that she was in her late twenties, but she surely was not going to invite jokes about it.

"Why do you feel he's road-weary?" she asked suddenly.

He thought before he answered.

"I think he really tries. But there is just no—spark. No life."

"Should there be?" asked Berta directly.

He turned to her as they continued down the walk. "Yes," he said with feeling. "Yes—there should be. If our religion, our faith, is really what we claim it is, then there should be. Plenty."

"What do you mean?"

"If we truly believe that God, the Creator, loved us even as sinful, destitute humanity, and loved us enough to send Christ, His Son, to redeem us from sin and set us on the right path—that He lives with us and in us as our Counselor and Guide—that He wants us at peace with ourselves and others, to express love and joy not just in our daily lives but in worship—then yes—there should be a spark—*life*."

He spoke with such fervor that Berta could only blink. She had never considered it before. Had never given thought to what she should expect from a morning in the worship service—from herself, from the pastor or the congregation. She had always gone to church. It was not just her right and privilege. It was her duty.

"But—" she began, then wasn't sure what she wanted to say in argument. His words made sense.

"Don't you believe it?" he asked.

"Believe what?" she countered.

"All that the church teaches?"

"Of course I believe it. You think me an infidel?"

"And you don't miss the—spark?"

She stopped and half turned to him. "Are you sure you aren't just a little bit—emotional? One's faith is not a—a giddy feeling. It's a commitment—a way of life."

"I'm not talking giddy," he responded. "And I am not criticizing our pastor—or what he preaches. He speaks the truth—but he does so with such—such control. Like he was giving a math equation. The Law of Gravity."

He paused beside her to press his point.

"And what, pray tell, are you suggesting he should do?" she asked him.

"*Sound* like he believes it. Exclaim over it. Rejoice about it. Get enthused. Why—he—he gives his sermon with less enthusiasm than I teach a history class."

Berta's mouth fell open. She couldn't believe that he would say such a thing about the pastor.

He flushed. "I'm sorry," he quickly apologized. "I shouldn't have said that. It—it sounds dreadfully disrespectful. Critical. I had no business getting so carried away. It's just—just that I go to church wanting—*longing* to rejoice in my salvation—and—and—" He stopped and shook his head. "I'm sorry," he said again. "I should not have brought it up."

They began to walk again. In silence now. But Berta's thoughts were whirling around in her head. It was the truth. The pastor did seem near exhaustion. How could he preach with enthusiasm when he appeared so tired? "Road-weary." Had they pushed him too hard for too long? How could he give to others what he did not himself possess? Why had she never thought of it? Why had she been content to just make her weekly appearance at church? Where was the life Thomas was talking about?

Chapter Sixteen

Jamie

Glenna's second baby, a girl, was named Berta Rosemary, and they called her Rosie. From the beginning, big brother Jamie adored her. He called her Sister and was the first to coax a smile from the infant.

"I think she likes me," he proudly informed his Aunt Berta one Sunday morning when they met at church.

"Of course she does," agreed Berta. She didn't say what she really felt in her heart. That no one could help liking the young Jamie. Berta still resisted openly showing affection for her nephew. She felt there was safety in holding the small boy at arm's length. She continued her stern, no-nonsense approach, but if Jamie noticed the distance, he never let it bother him. Warm, affectionate, giving, he was much like his mother. Berta felt the need both to protect him from future hurt by those who might take advantage of his good nature and to keep him from becoming too self-confident because of never being in conflict with others. It was a strange combination. Berta had a hard time keeping it all in balance.

"Do you love me, Aunt Berty?" Jamie surprised her by asking next.

"What makes you ask such a question?" she responded a little stiffly.

"I wonnered," he replied simply.

"One shouldn't fish for compliments—or for avowals," she said, nudging him toward the sanctuary door.

Jamie's expression indicated he had no idea what his Aunt Berta was saying, but he seemed to fully accept her just as she was. Stern and often reprimanding, yet at times affirming and supportive, the child seemed to be sure of her love whether or not she answered the question.

"Sister's too little to sit with us," Jamie explained, taking her hand and looking up into her face.

Berta nodded. Jamie still liked to sit with her in church.

"Someday she'll be big enough," he continued as though making excuses for the wee baby.

"Maybe she'll never wish to sit with us," Berta said rather abruptly. She was sure that she wouldn't appeal much to little girls. And Glenna's little girl was bound to be all softness and femininity. All laughter and giggles. All ribbons and lace.

"Sure she will," argued Jamie with confidence. "She likes me."

But will she like me? Berta could have asked but did not. There was no use trying to explain such complicated, grown-up things to the small boy.

They went in and took their places. From across the aisle Thomas gave Berta a good-morning nod. They never sat together in church. She had firmly stated that folks would misconstrue the action. She returned his nod without a smile and seated Jamie properly on the seat beside her. She smoothed out her skirt and picked up the hymnal to be ready for the opening song.

Pastor Jenkins took his place. He sat in the straight-backed chair, his face solemn, his eyes on his polished shoes.

He does look tired, Berta found herself thinking. *Something like Miss Phillips.*

Strange that she should think of Miss Phillips. The two were so totally different. Yet there were similarities. They were both pale. Listless. Neither one "mixed" a good deal. The pastor had once been a good socializer in the community, but since he had lost his wife he seemed to stay at home—shut in by himself. Berta suddenly wondered if he ate proper meals, or if, like Miss Phillips, he merely snacked—if he ate at all.

I wonder what we've been doing for him since Mrs. Jenkins died? she asked herself. She had not given the man much consideration until Thomas had brought up the subject. *Surely there are those in the congregation who are caring for the pastor,* Berta's thoughts continued. The elders. The deacons. Someone must be concerned about his welfare. As a single woman she could hardly be expected to entertain the widowed pastor.

He stood and announced the first hymn of the morning. Berta turned to the page and shared her book with Jamie even though he could not read one word from it.

Her thoughts turned from the minister to the service at hand. There wasn't anything different about the morning from any other Sunday. The events of the program proceeded just as she had grown to expect.

But at the end of the service her mind was jarred to attention. Deacon Burns stepped forward after the last hymn, cleared his throat, toyed with his rimmed spectacles, and began to speak.

"It is with deep regret that the Board of Elders has accepted the resignation of our pastor of thirty-seven years."

A hush fell over the entire congregation. It was followed by a low moan from Mrs. Tinker, who expressed all of her feelings by varying tones.

"Pastor Jenkins has handed us his resignation to be effective at the end of the month. He will be taking leave of his responsibilities in order to seek rest and restoration.

"Pastor Jenkins has served us long and well, and we are sorry to see him go. But we do believe—" He stopped and cleared his throat again. "We believe that he has earned the rest—that he needs the restoring. It has been difficult for him to carry on the ministry alone after the death of his dear wife two years ago. She has been deeply and sorely missed."

Again a moan from Mrs. Tinker.

"The elders will be actively searching for a replacement for our dear pastor. We would ask for your prayers—in regards to the search for the right minister to fill this pulpit—and for Pastor Jenkins as he seeks what God has for him in the future."

Another moan. This one low and long, a sign of Mrs. Tinker's deepest emotional distress.

Berta could not believe her ears. A new minister? She had never in her entire life had any minister but Pastor Jenkins. She couldn't imagine a worship service without the good man standing behind the pulpit. She wondered if she would even wish to attend on Sunday mornings with someone new representing the Lord.

Thomas would find my attitude shocking, she found herself thinking and wondered why Thomas and his response had popped into her mind.

"What did he say?" It was Jamie, tugging at her Sunday suit jacket and trying to keep his voice to a whisper.

Berta gave him a stern look and a caution to be quiet. She bent to him and whispered in his ear, "Pastor Jenkins will be leaving."

"Why? I like him," said the youngster.

"Shh. We all like him," replied Berta.

The congregation was stirring about now. The pastor had gone down the aisle to take his customary place at the door, greeting his congregation and receiving their regrets about his departure.

"Why?" asked Jamie in a rather loud whisper.

"He's tired," Berta whispered back. "He needs a rest."

"Like Mama?" asked Jamie, used to being cautioned to allow his mother to rest since the arrival of little Rosie.

"Sort of," replied Berta in a normal tone now that their discussion was covered by sounds of the people leaving the building. She began to gather her things together.

"I'm gonna miss church," said Jamie at her elbow. "I liked the stories and everything."

"We'll still have church," Berta was quick to tell him. He looked surprised.

"Who'll talk?" he asked her. "Mr. Burns?"

"We'll find another minister."

"When?"

"As soon as we can."

"I don't think I'll like him much," said Jamie stubbornly. "He won't be the same."

"No," agreed Berta shaking her head as she led the young boy from the pew. "He won't be the same." She looked down at Jamie beside her, a bit nonplussed that he had put her thoughts into words.

"Can I see you—in private?"

Thomas stood before her, his eyes shadowed. Berta could sense bad news, though she knew not why.

"What is it?" she asked sharply.

He nodded his head toward the small private room behind her.

Wordlessly she got up and led the way, fear and anger mingling within her. Why didn't he just say what was wrong?

"Is it Mama?" she asked as he closed the door firmly behind them.

He shook his head. "Jamie," was all he said.

Berta stood motionless. Her thoughts began to whirl. Jamie? Jamie wasn't sick. He was young—and strong. What possibly could have happened to Jamie?

Hands were easing her into a chair, gently but firmly. She wanted to strike out—to make him back off and leave her alone so she could sort it out.

"He fell—from a tree," he said.

"What—" she demanded.

"He's been taken to the hospital. Glenna is there. She sent word to me to come for you."

Berta's muddled head began to clear. Had Jamie broken an arm? A leg? Children were always breaking limbs. They healed quickly. She felt a measure of relief.

"They aren't sure of the injuries," Thomas was saying.

"What injuries?" she asked dumbly, panic again overtaking her.

"They don't know," continued Thomas. "He hurt his head—seriously. They don't know—"

But she stopped him with a swift backhand that caught him across the chest. She wrenched herself free from him and stood to her feet. "Don't talk nonsense," she declared. "His father's a doctor."

For a moment Thomas's eyes reflected surprise, then he seemed to understand.

"Of course," he agreed. "He'll get the best of care."

Berta headed for the door. He reached out and took her arm.

"Berta," he said, "Berta—"

"I need to get back to work," she said firmly, frowning at his hand on her arm.

"No," he said just as firmly. "No, you don't need to go back to work. I came to take you to the hospital. Glenna needs you."

She stared at him.

"I'll talk to Miss Phillips—tell her you are leaving. You get your things," he instructed.

She stared back at him, her eyes and throat dry. Was it really that serious—or was Glenna just suffering mother-panic?

Surely not Jamie. Not Jamie, her heart was crying, but she couldn't voice the words. Couldn't even let herself feel them.

"Is it necessary?" she managed to ask Thomas.

He nodded. "He's hurt quite badly, Berta."

She did not nod. Did not try to speak. Mutely and dumbly she moved toward her light shawl and hat. By habit, she placed the hat on her smoothly pinned hair. Reached for her gloves and moved woodenly through the door. The next thing she knew they were moving out of the building toward a waiting team and buggy.

Surely, this is all wrong. It's just a nightmare. It's not Jamie. It can't be Jamie. Her scattered thoughts kept fighting against the truth as they rode quickly through the streets.

Thomas helped her from the buggy and led her into the stark, sterile building. Down one hall and then another, around a corner, into a dark room, beyond that to another room, another hall. She did not understand where they were going, but she could fight against it no longer. It must be true. Jamie had been seriously hurt.

She heard a cry, "Oh, Berta," and Glenna threw herself into her arms. Berta mechanically put her arms around her younger sister and tried to calm her uncontrolled sobs.

"Shh. Shh," Berta said again and again as she held her. "It'll be all right. It'll be all right."

But Berta had no idea if her words were true.

When Glenna calmed enough to speak she sobbed out the story, as though she had to say it all to make it real. "He was climbing. That tree in the garden—after his kitten. He slipped and fell. He hit his head on a rock and—and—" She began to weep again.

Berta felt her anxiety being replaced by anger. *Why had they let Jamie climb the tree? Why hadn't someone been watching the boy? What kind of mother was Glenna—?*

But immediately she knew she wasn't being fair. No mother could protect a child twenty-four hours a day.

"Does Mama know?" she asked Glenna.

"Thomas has gone to her."

It was the first Berta realized that Thomas had left them. Distractedly, she wondered when he had slipped away.

Glenna was wiping at tears that streamed down her cheeks. "We need prayer," she whispered through trembling lips. "Lots of prayer. Parker says that only a miracle—"

Surely not, thought Berta. *He's a doctor. What did he train for if he couldn't do anything? He's supposed to be able to fix things,* she mentally accused.

"I asked our neighbor boy to run to Pastor Jenkins," Glenna told her. "He'll ask Deacon Burns to get the word out to the congregation. We need to pray." Glenna almost fell back into the chair behind her and bowed her tear-streaked face into her hands to resume praying.

Berta lowered herself slowly into the chair beside her. She felt helpless. Wooden. She should pray. Glenna was counting on her.

But she couldn't pray. She couldn't think. All she could do was moan. An image of Mrs. Tinker flashed into her mind. She understood her for the first time. Some things were felt far too deeply to be expressed in words— even in prayer.

———

The hours in the hospital corridor dragged slowly by. Pastor Jenkins came with his Bible and sympathy. Thomas finally returned with Mrs. Berdette. They huddled together, weeping and praying. Now and then Parker came out to Glenna or sent word with another doctor or a nurse. Berta couldn't understand the words. The talk. Her mind refused to accept anything that was being said.

It cannot be. It must not be. It is not my Jamie they are talking about. It was not Glenna's little boy who was hanging on to life by a thread. Surely his doctor father would be able to do something.

All through the long night Berta agonized. With all her heart she longed for the morning. *With morning this will all pass away,* she told herself. *Things will straighten out in the morning. They'll know what to do for him, come morning. Things are always more easily understood by the light of day*, she reassured herself.

"Would you like to see him?"

Parker stood by her side, looking exhausted. He still wore hospital whites and his surgical mask had slipped down haphazardly, covering his Adam's apple rather than his nose and mouth.

Berta was about to say no, then she realized that she

could not. She had to see him. She knew that. She stood unsteadily to her feet. Someone was taking her elbow, steering her down a long, empty hall. It was not Parker. He was on her other side.

Berta walked on, her legs rubbery, her mind in a haze. They passed through a door and into a brightly lit room. On the hospital table a small form was bundled. Bandages and tubes filled her with nameless dread. She didn't understand what they represented, and she realized she didn't wish to know either.

They moved her closer, almost against her will, and then she was looking down upon the face of little Jamie. He was so pale, so lifeless. So little.

A sob broke from Berta's lips. She caught herself before another could escape from her.

She stood for a moment with eyes closed, her mind and emotions reeling from shock and sorrow, and then she took hold of herself. She determinedly opened her eyes again, pushed back whoever was supporting her, leaned over the little boy and said in a firm, nearly calm voice, "Jamie. Jamie, listen to me. You get better. Do you hear? Rosie—"

For a moment she choked and could not go on, but she fought for control again. "Rosie needs her big brother. She likes you best. Remember?"

But she did not say the words that were in her heart. The words that she ached to say. *Jamie, I love you. I love you. Yes. The answer's yes—I love you.*

There was not even a twitch or a blink in response to her voice. Slowly she straightened, turned, and left the room.

It wasn't even a half hour later that a heartbroken Parker returned with the news that little Jamie was gone.

Chapter Seventeen

Strength

The months that followed were bleak and empty. Berta wished she could hide from the entire world. She wanted to shut herself away, close her eyes, stop her ears, and deny that it had ever happened. The deep, dark pain she was feeling was almost more than she could bear. Surely it too was as unreal as the tragedy itself.

But to any observers around her she carried on as usual. Berta was the strength for her mother, who grieved openly for her first grandchild, the small grandson she had lost. She was her sister's support and comforter as Glenna mourned the loss of her son. Berta continued doing what needed to be done, caring for the things that needed to be cared for, going through the motions of being alive.

"Berta is so strong," members of the congregation said often.

"I don't know what the family would do without Berta," community people said to one another.

And then the family was dealt a second blow. Granna passed away in her sleep. Another grave was prepared in the little churchyard cemetery.

"Can she be right beside Jamie?" asked Glenna, her voice breaking. "He seems so little to be left all alone there."

Berta thought she'd never be able to go through another family funeral, but the sight of her mother, shoulders bent, face pale and wan, made her straighten her back with determination. Her mother needed her as never before.

It was Glenna who seemed to work her way through the grief first. Berta wondered how she could still smile after what she had been through, but gentle, loving Glenna seemed even more joyous than she had been before.

It puzzled Berta. At times it even angered her. She found herself drawing away from Glenna. How could his own mother forget little Jamie so quickly and carry on with life as though—as though he had never existed?

Of course, there was small Rosie. Glenna seemed to take special delight in Rosie. But to Berta, the little girl with her smiles and coos was just a painful reminder of Jamie, who had loved her so.

And then Glenna was pregnant again. That, too, bothered Berta. Was Glenna trying to get a replacement for Jamie? Didn't she know that Jamie could not be replaced? There would never be another child like Jamie. Never.

The pain and anger twisted and turned within Berta, making her more and more withdrawn. More and more angry with life. And even angrier with God.

———

The church was having trouble finding a man to replace Pastor Jenkins. Much to the appreciation of the little congregation, the kind man agreed to stay on until a replacement could be found.

"Oh, I'm so glad," said Glenna with deep feeling. "We need a minister so much right now."

Berta frowned.

"I don't know how I would have ever made it through the—dark days—without Pastor Jenkins and his prayers," Glenna explained.

Berta said nothing.

Tears gathered in Glenna's eyes.

"Oh, Berta," she said, dabbing at the tears. "Some days I miss him so, I just—ache all over."

Berta still did not speak.

"Pastor said that we all—grieve in our own way. That we find healing at different speeds. The process has been a slow—and painful one for me. I sometimes wonder if I'll ever really feel whole again," continued Glenna.

Berta swallowed her unkind words. She wished to say that Glenna, with her chortling toddler Rosie, and her new baby on the way, seemed to be doing just fine without Jamie.

"If it hadn't been—there were so many times that I— I didn't want to even go on. I just—just—longed to—to curl up and die," Glenna continued.

If Berta had not suffered so deeply herself she could not have understood Glenna's words. As it was, she felt her sister was expressing her own dark thoughts.

"So how did you—manage?" she finally muttered. She wished to say, *How could you appear so happy if you were so deeply sad?* but she feared that Glenna would not understand the words or the bitterness that edged them.

"God," breathed Glenna. "I have never felt God so— real. So close to me. It is as though—as though He has been right there beside me—holding me up. Helping me through each day. He is so close. So close."

That's odd, thought Berta. *I have always felt He was so far away. In fact, I've wondered if He was really there at all. . . .*

———

Thomas purchased an automobile, a no-nonsense dark Ford with a covered top.

"I didn't think you would want to ride in the open," he told Berta. She didn't even think to wonder why her wishes would be considered.

"I thought you might like to call on your mother," he went on. "It will take far less time by car than by buggy."

Berta knew that was so. She had ridden with Parker and Glenna on one of their trips to the farm. She had been amazed at how quickly Parker's automobile had covered the miles. Parker had purchased a car as soon as he could, since it would save him countless hours when calling on patients.

"It could mean the difference between life and death," he had told Glenna in Berta's hearing.

I don't know, thought Berta bitterly. *You were there with Jamie the total time, and it made no difference.* But Berta did not say the words.

Berta felt no interest nor attraction to cars. Not Parker's neat gray Hudson or Thomas's dark Ford, but she did agree that she should take a trip to check on her mother and it would be foolish to decline Thomas's offer.

"I'll get my things," she said in answer to his invitation.

"Be sure to bring a scarf for your head," he called after her. "It gets chilly."

Berta nodded as she walked away.

Berta was concerned as soon as she walked into the farm home. Things did not seem to be as they should. Her mother looked wan and listless.

"Mama," she coaxed. "You really shouldn't be staying here alone. Please—come into town with me."

But her mother shook her head stubbornly.

"I don't wish to interfere in your life, dear," she answered. "And really, I quite like it here. I'm familiar with every nook and cranny of this old house. I feel I belong here. I don't think I'd like the city."

"But you shouldn't be alone," argued Berta.

"And why not?"

"You're—not strong enough—anymore. You've been through so much the last months. Come with me until—until you get back on your feet again."

"I don't think so," the woman replied. "John will keep an eye on me. He's close-by."

"But John can't watch over you every minute. You could fall—or . . ."

"Or what? What's the worst that could possibly happen to me? Death? We all have to die."

"Mama, don't talk that way," cut in Berta sharply. "It's not—at all—proper."

Mrs. Berdette sighed. "You're right," she said. Berta saw tears in her eyes. "But I don't fear death like I once did. I don't even—dread it. Sometimes I think I might even welcome—"

"That's foolish talk," Berta interrupted again. It unnerved her to hear her mother saying such morbid things.

"Death is the only gate to heaven," her mother said frankly. "Why should we who are on the right path make such a fuss about walking through the gate?"

Berta did not wish to hear any more. "Won't you come?" she asked, trying to change the topic back to the present need.

"I don't think so. At least not yet. I want to stay right

here and watch spring come again. I always enjoy the springtime. So did Mama. I'm sorry she isn't here to see it this year."

She would soon be back to talking about death again. Berta did not want another little discourse on the topic.

"Well, we must get back to town before dark. If you won't come, then I guess I can't force you. But I do wish you would reconsider."

Mrs. Berdette shook her head. "I feel closer to—family when I'm here," she said simply.

Berta left, still agitated and anxious.

———————

They did finally find a new pastor. When she heard about it, Berta did not feel particularly enthusiastic or even curious. In fact, it had been some time since she had felt excited about church or anything else in her life.

With no emotion whatsoever, she settled herself in her familiar pew on his first Sunday. As she had come to do on every Sunday morning, she kept her eyes straight ahead, as though allowing them to turn to the empty place beside her would be a painful reminder that Jamie was still—and always would be—missing.

The energetic Rosie had never asked to sit with Aunt Berty. Berta doubted that she ever would. Rosie was not Jamie. Rosie never responded so warmly to her stern Aunt Berty as Jamie had done. The little girl was much too busy keeping her father and mother on the run to think about sitting with anyone.

Berta smoothed her skirt, picked up the hymnal, and disinterestedly watched the new man take his place on the familiar platform.

The service proceeded as usual. Deacon Burns introduced the new pastor with a great deal of fervor, about how God had led and assisted in the search for the right man, and his own confidence that such a man had been found. At last he turned the pulpit over to the new minister.

Berta was not listening too closely. Ever since they had lost Jamie, she had developed a bad habit of letting her Sunday thoughts wander to other things.

Her attention was suddenly jerked back to the present when she heard the man ask with forceful candor, "Why am I here?"

Concentrating on what he was saying, she heard, ". . . here because I believe in God."

That isn't really such a surprise, she reasoned.

"I believe in *a* God," the man went on, emphasizing the "a."

"I think it is perfectly reasonable to believe in a God. Not—many gods. Many gods would result in chaos. Lesser gods—greater gods—warring gods—self-seeking gods. Can you imagine such a world? It wouldn't work. If a god isn't really God of all—then he is no god at all. Therefore I believe in one God—*the* God—the reason for all that is and all that ever will be."

Berta shifted slightly and prepared to see where he was headed with these declarations.

"So—to me it has been settled. Forever. Clearly. I believe in one God—Creator and Sustainer of all things."

He stopped for a breath and glanced down at his open Bible.

"Since this Creator God has given us His Word, then it follows that I must also believe that the Bible—which tells us of Him—is truth. It is His revelation to mankind. The oldest and most accurate of religious documents—revealing who He is and what He stands for."

He held up the well-worn volume before him.

"So," he paused a moment, "I believe in one God—

Creator and Sustainer of all things, and I believe that the Bible is His revelation to mankind of who and what He is.

"If I believe the Bible is given by Him, and He is God—*the* God—then I must accept this Book as it is. All of it. To dissect it and choose this and throw out that would discredit it all. To pick my own passages to please my own theories or personal pet doctrines, or pattern my own philosophies or religion on what tickles my ears or pleases my fancy, and reject what else it says, would invalidate the whole. So I must believe and accept it *all*— for what it says throughout.

"Thus—I believe in one God—the God—One, though triune—Maker and Sustainer of all things.

"I believe the Bible is His revelation to mankind.

"I believe the Bible must be accepted and obeyed in its entirety. It is the written Word of God."

He paused and studied his congregation.

"So all my sermons will come directly from these pages." He held up his Bible again. "We will study together what the Word says. We will pray for understanding and His wisdom. We will pray for willingness to accept with open hearts and minds what that means for you—for me—in our everyday living.

"We face hard questions in our modern world—but the answers are here in this Book. To find the answers we must first know the Source—God. God the Father— who loves us. God the Son—who redeems us. God the Spirit—who leads us. One God, yet three in person—in workings, a mystery—beyond our human comprehension, but one God.

"Our purpose for meeting here from Sunday to Sunday is to get to know that God. To know Him better and better so that we can worship Him more fully.

"I am here to lead you in your search for God. That is

174

all. That is my sole reason for being here. To strengthen our understanding of God. But more than our understanding—our relationship. We want to go far beyond knowing *about* Him—we want to know *Him*. Together we will embark on that journey. May our hearts and minds be united as one as we begin our search.

"Before we start the journey together in the first chapter of Genesis, let's bow our heads and ask God to open our minds—and our hearts to the truth."

Berta bowed her head.

Something was stirring within her. A strange uneasiness tinged with excitement made her shift restlessly. God had been so far away recently. She had begun to doubt her own faith. Was it true what she had been taught since childhood? And now this man was saying that they were going to learn who God really was. To not only discover Him but to get to know Him intimately.

Did she want that? Did she dare seek God in such a way? What might it reveal about Him? About herself? How might it affect who she was?

She wished to turn and study the faces around her. Were her fellow worshippers affected by the words as she had been? Were they willing to search through the pages of the Bible to find out who and what God was?

She shifted the Bible she held in her own hands. Somehow she had the feeling that something was changing. If others were having a similar experience, if the wheels were really put in motion, this church might never be the same again.

———

Over the months that followed, the new pastor was true to his word. Sunday by Sunday, they turned together to the Word of God to see what it told them about who God was and how He wished to interact with fallen, then redeemed, mankind.

In spite of her reluctance to begin the journey, Berta found herself drawn in. She was making some amazing discoveries. She was seeing some wonderful spiritual truths. *Surely, surely,* she reasoned within herself, *they must have been there all the time. I thought I knew my Bible—but I just knew some of the facts. The stories. I had never really taken the facts—the truths—and applied them to myself, my own life, before.*

Berta began to wonder how she could have been brought up in the church and missed so much. *No wonder Glenna finds God close—and I felt He was so distant. Glenna knows God. I have been trying to muddle through life—just knowing about Him.*

It was an amazing discovery—but only the beginning.

Chapter Eighteen

Joseph

Berta now looked forward to Sunday. It was a new experience for her to awaken on Sunday morning anticipating worship. For so many years she had simply met with others in the little church because it was the thing to do. With her new discoveries, she could hardly wait for another Sunday.

Sermon by sermon the new pastor was taking his congregation through the Bible in their search to know God. Week by week Berta's eyes began to open. And as she understood more of God, she also understood more concerning herself.

"My, I've got a rebellious streak," she surprised herself by admitting aloud as she combed her hair before her large gilt mirror.

Glenna had commented on her hair the week before, telling Berta what a lovely color it was and suggesting that it would be very becoming pinned in the new fashion.

Berta had answered quite sharply, telling Glenna that her hair was just fine as it was, and she had no intention of changing her style just because it was "the new fashion."

Glenna had said no more, but Berta had seen the hurt in her eyes.

"Well, Lord," she spoke again. "I guess that's something else you and I will have to work on."

She pinned her hat over her hair with a firm, steady hand, surveyed herself briefly to make sure there were no loose ends to her hair or the rest of her appearance, picked up her things from the hall table, and briskly set off for church.

The sermon was an especially thought-provoking one. The pastor was well into the book of Genesis, and for three Sundays he had been speaking on the life of Joseph.

"What a series of events in the life of the man. His steps seemed to just keep going down, down, down. How could things get any worse for Joseph? How could the hand of God possibly be working for good in his life? But, remember," he cautioned, "we are looking at the external. Inwardly—spiritually—Joseph was not being trampled down. He was being built up. The very adversities that seemed certain to bring defeat, built inner strength instead—reliance and trust, a deep faith in his God."

Berta hung on every word of the message. Could God really be building on the inside at the same moment that the evil forces seemed to be tearing away at the outside? She pondered the question.

She shifted her position slightly and glanced toward Glenna. There sat her sister, a look of serenity and joy on her face as she held her new baby girl in her arms. Berta felt a twinge deep down inside. How could Glenna still smile? Berta knew she had loved Jamie deeply. She knew that her sister still spent times in weeping for his loss. Then, how?

The puzzling question had distracted Berta for a moment. She turned back to try to pick up on what the pastor was saying.

"Faith is broad. Faith is all-encómpassing. Faith is more than an acceptance of Christ's work on Calvary. Faith is a warm blanket to wrap us against the harsh cold of life's dark nights. Faith is belief that God knows exactly what He is doing and that He is in charge.

"Turn with me to Proverbs twenty-one, verse thirty."

The pastor thumbed through his Bible, and Berta heard the rustle of pages as many others found the passage also. She stared at him as he read, " 'There is no wisdom, no insight, no plan that can succeed against the Lord.'

"Do you believe that? Then you should feel like shouting, 'Hallelujah.' Hallelujah! God is in control. There is nothing that takes Him by surprise. There is no one who can outwit Him, outmaneuver Him, outdo Him, or outlast Him. He is *God*.

"That is what Joseph understood. That is why Joseph knew he was being built up in spirit during the seemingly worst events of his life."

Some things suddenly seemed to fall into place for Berta. She cast another glance at Glenna. *That's it,* she whispered to herself. *That's what Glenna understands. That's why.*

Berta lowered her head and fought against tears. It was a new and troubling experience. Berta had rarely allowed herself to cry since she had been a child. She swallowed the tears away with firm determination.

———

The beautiful autumn day and warm Indian summer sunshine with its teasing gentle breeze lent itself to ambling rather than walking at a brisk gait, and Berta and Thomas both seemed to sense its mood. They walked slowly, thinking more than talking. Berta's contemplations were still on the morning sermon and her discovery of what made her sister Glenna able to survive and even overcome a mother's nightmare.

She's always been that way, she mused to herself. *Always—sensitive, open.* Then Berta pushed the thought away. *Well—why not?* She was always the favored one—pampered because of her prettiness. It was easy for her to be good. She never had to fight for anything.

"Joseph was quite a man," Thomas's voice cut into her thoughts.

She nodded.

"Where do you think he came from?" asked Thomas.

Berta looked at him, not understanding his question. The pastor had spent many Sundays on the lineage of Joseph.

"I've been mulling that around for days," went on Thomas. "Where did he come from?"

"Rachel," said Berta abruptly.

"No. No—I don't mean physically," Thomas said quickly, then chuckled at Berta's terseness. "The *real* Joseph," he explained. "The one who responded fully to God. I mean—look at the man. His great-grandfather was Abraham. Called from an idolatrous nation. Abraham couldn't have known too much about the true God. He even responded to God's order to kill his son without question. Sure, he must have had questions about it—but he would have been familiar with human sacrifice, coming from where he did. I don't think it was the call of his God, whom he had learned to fully trust, to sacrifice that would have nearly—nearly undone him. It would have been the fact that God had promised this son and now He was asking for him back."

Berta had never considered the possibility that Abraham's past society, which had made human sacrifice a part of its culture, had played a significant role in his story.

"And this man, this Abraham *lied*. On more than one occasion he deceived—or tried to. Then we have Joseph's grandfather, Isaac—an unwise father who favored one son over the other. He and his wife played tug-of-war with their two offspring."

At Berta's quick look he hastily continued, "Oh, that might be a bit harsh. But they certainly were unwise parents. Then we go to Joseph's own family. Think of it. Jacob—the deceiver—for a father. And a house full of contentious, bickering women. Rachel and Leah—always trying to outsmart each other to get Jacob's attention. Seeking his favor. What kind of setting is that for a child? Favored son? That hardly stood him in good stead with the rest of the boys."

Berta could not help but smile.

"So where did he come from? A background of deceit and self-seeking. A household of contention and manipulation. What made Joseph a man who would face prison—or death—rather than shame his God?"

She shrugged. Berta had never thought about Joseph's home situation. Where had Joseph learned his morals, his values? Why did he have such strong convictions? Who had taught him right from wrong?

"To me, Joseph's story is so exciting," Thomas said. "To me it says that people do have equal chances. Just because your background is not ideal does not mean that you can't be a just person. I mean, God chose Abraham and brought him out of a heathen country because God saw he was a man He could work with. A man who could learn. Could yield. Not a perfect man—but a pliable one."

"You should have been a preacher," Berta said with a little smile.

Thomas smiled back but hurried on.

"And, Isaac and Jacob. They made mistakes—but God kept leading them on and they learned lessons too—sometimes the hard way.

"And then comes Joseph—and he really had a heart to learn—and just look what God was able to do with him."

Berta lifted her head to catch the song of a wren in a nearby tree.

"So it really comes right down to the individual," Thomas continued. "You can choose to listen—or you can shut God out. Circumstances—good or bad—don't necessarily make the man. Joseph could have been just like one of his—pitiful brothers. Murderous and deceitful. But he wasn't."

Berta felt a stirring deep down inside herself again. Did one really get to choose—or did circumstances dictate? It was a deep, troubling question and one that she did not wish to deal with on such a beautiful morning.

"That's an interesting idea," she said to Thomas, pushing the question aside. "And it needs a good deal of pondering, and today is too nice a day to be thinking deeply. I think I'll have a quick meal and go for a walk along the creek."

"Is it to be a soulful walk?" asked Thomas. "Or would you mind company?"

"You can come if you wish," replied Berta with no hesitation, her tone even.

"I'll do that," he replied.

They reached Berta's gate. She slowed her step.

"I could make a few sandwiches and we could eat along the stream," she offered.

He smiled.

"Sounds great. I'll hurry on home and change into more comfortable walking clothes. I could even make up some lemonade and bring some fruit."

Berta nodded. It seemed they were going to have an improvised picnic.

————————

The fall day could only be described as gorgeous. Already, colored leaves were lining the path, though the trees still carried many in their autumn dress.

"My favorite time of year," mused Berta.

"I think it's mine as well," observed Thomas. "I'm not sure why."

"I think it's because it always reminds me of the farm," Berta explained.

"Perhaps. For me—I guess it—speaks of God's care. There is the harvesting—the gardening—the fruit—all reminders of how He nurtures us, takes us into account."

Berta nodded, sighed deeply, and leaned back against the tree where they had spread the picnic blanket.

"I think it is one final gift from God before the bleakness of winter," she said.

Thomas looked at her in surprise. "You don't like winter?"

She shrugged. "I don't dislike winter. It's just that it's so cold and harsh and harder to do—whatever you do. And you have to stay in more and—" She came to a halt. "Come to think of it," she said with a chuckle, "I don't mind it at all. I like the warm fires in the hearth and the song of the kettle on the back of the kitchen stove."

"The faint smell of woodsmoke in the crisp air," added Thomas.

"I like to curl up with a book by the fire, a warm shawl draped over my shoulders," went on Berta.

"The sight of large, fluffy snowflakes drifting silently down to cover all of the drabness and clutter of the world."

"The sounds that seem to ring out for miles on a clear day—children shouting—sleigh bells ringing—the train whistle as it rounds the bend way over in the gulch," added Berta.

"And the crunch of snow underfoot as you walk. Or the swish of sled runners as you fly down a hill," said Thomas.

They laughed together. Winter wasn't so bad after all.

"Are you busy tonight?" It was Berta who asked the question. Thomas glanced down at the book he had just selected from the library shelf, then back at her.

"No—I'm free," he answered.

"I was thinking that I should go to see Mama. It's been a while since I've been out. I wondered if you'd drive me."

"Certainly," responded Thomas quickly.

"I'd like to leave right after work," Berta told him.

"I'll go get the car," replied Thomas, who always walked to the library.

"Thank you," said Berta and turned back to tidying the librarian's desk. Miss Phillips was home with a cold, so Berta had the work to do alone.

It was not long before Thomas was waiting in front of the door. Berta could hear the Ford motor running.

It will be a chilly ride, she thought to herself. *I'm glad I dressed warmly when I left home this morning.*

They spoke little on the way to the farm. Thomas inquired about her mother, and Berta replied that she didn't really know—it had been too long since she had made a visit. She was ashamed of her neglect.

But when they arrived at the farm they found Mrs. Berdette busily engaged in her kitchen. She was pleased to see them and invited them in to the warmth of the fire.

"I was just fixing a bowl of hot soup," she said. "I'm glad I made enough for two cold, hungry travelers."

She laughed softly.

"So what brings you out on such a chilly night?" she went on.

"I wanted to see how you are," replied Berta. "It has been some time since I've been out. I was afraid that you would feel I had forgotten you."

"Glenna and Parker have been here several times," said Mrs. Berdette. "My, she has a pair of sweet little girls. I just enjoy them so. Sometimes I wish I was closer so that . . ." Her voice drifted to a stop.

"So why don't you?" urged Berta. "Why won't you move into town with me. You know I've—"

"I know. I know," replied Mrs. Berdette. "But I—" she stopped again.

"You what?" prompted Berta.

"Well I—I don't want to—get in your way."

"In my way? What do you mean, in my way? You know I'd love to have you and—"

"I know." Mrs. Berdette cast a glance toward Thomas. She hesitated.

"So what—?" began Berta.

"Well—it just doesn't seem right for a mother to be hanging around when her daughter has a—suitor," finished Mrs. Berdette quickly with another glance toward Thomas.

Berta's face colored, then paled. After an initial look of shock she plunged forward.

"Mama—Thomas is not my suitor."

Mrs. Berdette looked doubtful.

"He's not," declared Berta.

"Does Thomas know that?" asked Mrs. Berdette with a little smile as she lowered herself to a kitchen chair.

Berta became more flustered. She stood quickly. "Of course," she replied. "We discussed it frankly—openly—with each other. We do not wish a—a—anything more than friendship. We have agreed."

Mrs. Berdette still looked doubtful. She looked to Thomas, who made no comment but simply watched Berta's face.

———

It was a quiet ride home. Berta was wrapped in her own thoughts. She did wish that her mother would listen to reason. Would not be so stubborn. A suitor. Indeed! Such a ridiculous idea.

She cast a glance toward Thomas, who was paying particularly close attention to the road. He seemed to feel her eyes on him and turned slightly to look at her. She flushed at having been caught studying his face.

"Mama," she said to cover her embarrassment. "I wish she wasn't so—so set. So—opinionated. I don't think she believed me even when I told her—"

"Berta," said Thomas softly. "I did not wish to contradict your words—but—" He stopped, as though uncertain how to continue.

"We *have* agreed to friendship," he finally went on.

"That's what I said," Berta reminded him.

He nodded. "But it isn't what we both—wish," he said quietly.

She looked at him, not understanding his comment.

"I cannot be less than honest," he said evenly. "We promised to always be truthful with each other."

Berta nodded.

"I—agreed to friendship. But I still—with all my heart—wish our relationship—was more."

The words hung in the silence between them. The chugging of the Ford engine was the only sound on the stillness.

"Oh, Thomas," groaned Berta finally. "Please don't go and spoil things."

Chapter Nineteen

Library Woes

Berta awakened from a sound sleep to hear someone running along the sidewalk. She shifted uneasily in her bed, straining to hear anything further. Then there was a pounding on her door.

She threw back her covers and thrust her feet to the floor rug. Without stopping for her slippers, she grabbed her robe and wrapped it about her as she hastened toward the door.

Mama, was her immediate thought.

A man that she did not know stood on her step. His shoulders were rising and falling with each breath that he took, the little streams of steam puffing out on the crisp night air.

Berta opened her mouth to ask his mission when he blurted out, "The library's burnin'."

"Burning?"

Berta, not believing the man, leaned from her door and looked toward the section of town where the library had stood for many years. There was a bright glare in the night sky. Suddenly she realized that she smelled smoke.

"What happened?" she demanded.

"No one knows—yet," the man replied. "They just told me to fetch ya."

"What on earth can I do?" asked Berta frankly. "Have they called the fire engine?"

"Fire fighters are already there," he panted, about to bolt again. He was missing all the action.

"How bad is it?" Berta asked quickly, not wanting him to get away before she had as much information as possible.

"Pretty bad," he said and turned to go. "Better see for yourself," he flung back over his shoulder.

In her anxiety, Berta almost forgot to close the door. Hurriedly she dressed and left her little house at a run.

Ahead she could see the glow of fire reflected in the night sky, though she could not see actual flames.

"Whatever happened?" she asked herself over and over as she ran.

She turned the corner to see a tower of flames. The smoke nearly choked her, even at this distance.

It seemed that the whole town was there. People were shifting and scurrying and rushing about. The fire engine was indeed there. Black-clothed firemen manned a hose that kept sending arcs of water into the hissing flames.

They'll never save it. They'll never save it, Berta's thoughts whirled. *All our books—gone. Whatever will we do?*

She felt a sickness deep inside, and for a moment she wondered if she was going to vomit. With all her will she fought against it and finally managed to get control of herself.

Someone pulled on her coat sleeve, and she turned to see Miss Phillips at her elbow.

It was hard to speak. The roar of the flames, the noise of the fire truck, and the shouts of people drowned out one's own voice. The smoke was so thick that Berta avoided taking a deep breath. She moved her head closer to Miss Phillips to try to catch the words from the pale, tight lips.

"It's gone," the woman said pathetically. "Gone."

Her words were so mournful—so totally without hope. Berta instinctively reached out and placed an arm about the older woman. "You should go home," she said, leaning to speak in her ear. "You can't do anything here. You should go home."

Miss Phillips began to tremble.

"Come on," said Berta. "I'll take you home."

She didn't know where Miss Phillips lived. She was hoping that the stricken woman would be alert enough to find the way.

"It's gone. All gone," Miss Phillips kept mumbling as Berta led her down the street away from the burning building.

"Miss Phillips—we must get you home," Berta said, giving the woman's shoulder a little squeeze. "Where do you live?"

They turned the corner. The noise and smoke lessened.

"Miss Phillips," Berta said again, stopping the woman. "You need to get inside. Where do you live?"

The woman only looked more bewildered.

"Your home? Where do you live? Think," Berta commanded.

"I—I—" The woman began to look around in confusion.

"Can't you remember? Think. Where do you live?" asked Berta again.

The woman started walking. Berta pulled her heavy coat more tightly about her and followed along in the bitter cold.

They stumbled their way along the snowy street. *I hope we get there soon,* thought Berta. *I'm about to freeze.* She looked at Miss Phillips. She was wearing only a light coat over her flannel nightgown. Berta noticed that she had on only house slippers. *She'll freeze to death before I can get her in,* thought Berta.

Suddenly Miss Phillips stopped and looked around again, her face blank.

"Miss Phillips—we must get you in out of the cold," said Berta.

"I—I don't understand," mumbled Miss Phillips. "It was right here."

"What was right here?"

Miss Phillips looked around her, fear now showing in her face.

"I used to live on this street," she said to Berta, "until someone moved it."

"Moved it?"

"My house—it's gone. I don't know what they've done with it," the woman continued in a bewildered voice. "Used to be here—somewhere."

Fear gripped Berta's heart. Miss Phillips was totally confused.

"Come," said Berta. "I'll take you home to my house. We must get indoors before you freeze."

But the older woman resisted her help, pulling against Berta's gentle tug.

"Please, Miss Phillips," Berta pleaded, "please come with me."

"It's all gone," Miss Phillips was saying again.

"We'll find it," replied Berta. "You come with me and we'll find it—together. Please, Miss Phillips. Come along with me."

The older woman still resisted, but she did allow Berta to draw her along through the streets until she came to her own little gate. Berta's teeth were chattering and her shoulders trembling from the cold as she coaxed her numb fingers to open the door.

"Now, Miss Phillips—you sit right here," Berta said, lowering the woman to a chair. "I'll stir up the fire. We'll soon be thawed out."

Berta tried to hurry. She had to get the banked fire coaxed into flame. She crouched before the fireplace and began to blow on the log.

"It's all gone," murmured Miss Phillips. "The books— my room. It's all gone."

A little flame quickened. Berta took heart and placed some small kindling near the flickering coals.

The next thing she knew she was flat on her back. Miss Phillips had caught her completely off guard and given her a shove with strength that Berta never guessed she had. The elderly woman now stood over her, a look of panic on her face. "The fire," she cried wildly, pointing at the small flame. "It's here now! We'd better run." And she made a dash for Berta's door.

"No," cried Berta, scrambling to her feet. "No—don't go."

She managed to stop the woman before she fled the house, but Miss Phillips still kept staring at the fireplace with fear in her eyes.

"I won't start the fire," said Berta. "We'll just leave it. Come. Come to the kitchen."

She half pulled the woman through the door into the little kitchen, carrying the lamp in one hand so they could see their way. There was still warmth in the room from the banked kitchen range.

"Sit here," Berta commanded, easing the woman into a kitchen chair.

Berta crossed to the kitchen stove and turned her back to shield the range from the woman as she lifted the stove lid. The fire had not gone out. With her body still hiding the flames from the woman, Berta covertly added a few pieces of wood to the fire box. She prayed that the smoldering coals would soon light the wood.

"I smell smoke," Miss Phillips said in panic, and Berta quickly dropped the stove lid into place and whirled, ready to protect her frightened guest again.

"Sit down, Miss Phillips," she ordered sternly. To her surprise the woman obeyed, but she was still sniffing the air.

"I'm going to fix us tea," said Berta.

"It's all gone," the woman mourned, shaking her head sadly.

She lowered her face into her hands and began to sob. Berta crossed to her and put an arm around the thin, shaking shoulders.

"It'll be all right, Miss Phillips," she comforted as she drew the woman close and patted her shoulder. "It'll be all right. They'll take care of it."

But Berta wasn't sure it would be done in time to be of help to Miss Phillips. The woman seemed to be totally out of her mind.

Berta was relieved to hear the teakettle finally begin to sing. She set about preparing the tea while Miss Phillips sat in the kitchen chair, rocking back and forth, her eyes unfocused. "It's gone," she kept mumbling. "Everything's gone."

Someone knocked. Berta cast a glance at Miss Phillips, then another at her kitchen door. It was secured with a bolt. Still, she was afraid that the woman might somehow be able to pull the bolt and dash off into the night while Berta answered the front door.

"Someone is knocking," she said to the woman. "Let's go see who it is."

Miss Phillips looked hesitant.

"Come," said Berta, pulling her to her feet. "We must answer the door."

"No," the woman responded sharply, jerking her arm from Berta's hold. "Mama said never to open the door at night."

Berta looked at her. The woman stared back, a look of confusion on her face.

"It is night—isn't it?" she inquired of Berta.

"Yes. Yes—it is."

The knock came again—more insistent this time. Berta cast a glance around her, then made her decision. She would run to the door and hope with all her heart that Miss Phillips would stay put.

"You wait," she flung over her shoulder as she hurried out.

Parker stood on the step. Berta was never so glad to see anyone in her life.

"Come in," she urged him, anxious to close the door and get back to the kitchen.

"We were worried about you," Parker said. "Someone told us they'd seen you at the fire—then didn't know where you'd gone."

"It's Miss Phillips," said Berta, leading the way to the kitchen. "I'm afraid she is—" She stopped and looked at him. "I know nothing of these things, Parker," she whispered, "but I think she's—lost her mind."

"Shock?" he asked her as they started toward the kitchen again.

Miss Phillips was still in the kitchen chair. She continued to rock back and forth, a wild look on her face. When she saw Parker she looked ready to bolt again.

"Did *you* take it?" the agitated woman asked him.

Parker crossed to her and reached a hand out to touch her shoulder.

"Miss Phillips," he said in a soft, reassuring tone.

"Miss Phillips—your books will be just fine. The firemen are taking good care of them."

"Did you take it?" she repeated.

"Did you lose something?" asked Parker gently.

For a moment she seemed perplexed. Then she let her gaze sweep over the kitchen.

"I used to live here," she tried to explain. "But they've changed it. My—my blue pillow—it's gone."

"We'll find it," promised Parker. "You come with me and—"

"She's half-frozen," Berta explained. "I was just fixing her tea. Would you like a cup?"

Parker nodded. "Sounds good," he said. "I'm about beat."

He looked carefully at Miss Phillips. "While you're doing that I'll slip out for my medical bag," Parker said softly. "I've some tablets I think might help her until I get her to the hospital for care. I'll just pop one in her tea."

Berta looked at the older woman. She had put her face in her hands again, still rocking back and forth in the chair. Berta could hear her mumbling, but she couldn't understand the words.

———

In the morning Berta dreaded going out to face the day. She especially hated to make the walk to the library. What was left? Anything? She'd had no report. She had no idea what she would find.

Just as she stepped from her door, Thomas pulled up in the Ford.

"I thought you might like a ride this morning," he called to her.

Berta had no intention of arguing.

"I hear you had quite a night," he said as he helped her into the car.

She nodded.

"Have you heard any word—about Miss Phillips?" she asked him.

"Saw Parker. He says that the poor old soul isn't in very good shape. Complete shock. She's still totally confused. If it hadn't been for you last night she likely would have died of cold, out on the street."

Berta brushed that aside with a little gesture. "The poor thing," she said. "The library has been her life."

Thomas nodded. He turned to her.

"And you?" he asked. "How are you faring?"

Berta paused. She still hadn't had a chance to work it all out in her thinking.

"I—honestly don't know," she responded. "I've no idea what I'll find."

"There is still a library," he informed her. "The firemen were able to put out the flame before it was totally destroyed. But—I don't think you will be working in it this morning. It's quite a mess."

Thomas's words had not prepared her for what they found. Everything was ice-covered from the night before. The blackened bricks of the library front were brightened only where stout boards had been nailed across the gaping windows. Even the door was gone—replaced by heavy boards.

"It—it looks terrible," murmured Berta under her breath.

Thomas pulled up before the building and let Berta study the damage. But before she could get out of the car he spoke again.

"I thought you'd need to see it," he said. "But you won't be working. Mayor Henderson said for you to pay a visit to his office. He'll discuss with you the future plans."

Berta nodded. She didn't wish to look at the charred and scarred building any longer.

"Let's go," she replied stiffly.

Thomas moved the car out into the street and toward City Hall.

Mayor Henderson was blustering about the office as they entered.

"Miss Berdette," he said when he saw Berta. "Terrible thing. Terrible thing—losing our library."

He clicked his tongue and shook his head as though he was still in a state of shock.

"Come in. Come in," he invited. "We need to work some things out."

"You don't need to wait," Berta informed Thomas.

He nodded. "I do have a class to teach," he admitted.

"Thank you—for coming for me," she said wearily, and she turned to follow the fussy little mayor into his office.

"Terrible thing. Terrible thing," he was still exclaiming.

They spent a good deal of the morning discussing the library and what could be done in the future. They both knew that Berta would not be able to start any work of salvaging books at the present site, since there was no way of heating the building. Berta had no idea what she might find anyway. She dreaded the task ahead.

"I think I'll send a crew over to haul all the books into that vacant building just down the street," the mayor said. "That way you can start some sorting before the building is repaired. They have assured me that the building can be repaired. The structure still seems sound enough. But it's going to take time—yes, ma'am, it's going to take time."

Berta nodded. She knew she should feel pleased that she still had a job.

She left the mayor with his promise that he would send word to her as soon as the books had been moved. She could then begin her sorting to see what could be salvaged.

Berta started the long walk home.

The smell of smoke still hung heavily in the air. Berta hated it. It was a reminder of all that had been lost to the flames. *Poor Miss Phillips,* she thought silently. She wondered if the woman would ever be the same again. She hoped with all her heart that the confusion would not be permanent.

Chapter Twenty

Back on Track

A week later Berta shook her head as she looked around the room stacked with boxes of books from the library. The acrid smell of smoke had come with the books even after being relocated to another building.

"I don't know where to start." With a sigh Berta crossed to hang up her coat. At least the room was comfortably warm.

I should have worn my oldest garden clothes, she observed as she leaned over the box closest to her and lifted back the flaps. The books she could see were covered with soot and messy with water damage.

Oh, dear, I hope they aren't all like this—we'll save very little at this rate.

Grimacing against the grime and smell, she started in on the first box.

She was right. By the time she had sorted through the entire box of books, she had found two that would still be usable. Even they smelled strongly. The other ones were either charred or water-soaked from the fire fighters' hoses.

All through the long morning Berta worked, bending

over boxes, sorting books into piles, writing notes in her pad of paper. It appeared there would be far more books to be replaced than there would be books that could be put back on the shelves.

As time wore on, Berta fretted that they should just dispose of the whole mess and start over. But she knew that would not be reasonable. The town had been so proud of their library and its collection. They had spent many years building it to what it was. Now they had little left to show for their efforts. But what could be reclaimed would be some small victory.

This is even worse than I had imagined, mourned Berta as the day wore on. Already her back complained, her head ached, and her clothes were filthy. She looked down at her blackened hands. She wondered if they would ever come clean again.

Thomas stopped by on his way home from the university.

"How is it going?" he asked her, his tone sympathetic.

"It's really quite horrible," she answered with a grimace. "What isn't burned is water damaged."

"That's often the worst part of a fire," he observed.

"Well, I've just gotten started—but I sure haven't found many that we can use," said Berta. "It's most discouraging."

"I think you've worked long enough for one day," said Thomas. "Why don't you get your coat."

Berta looked down at her soiled hands. "I hate to touch anything with—these," she answered.

"Where's your coat? I'll get it."

Berta nodded toward the closet and went to attempt washing the worst of the soot from her hands. It had worked itself all the way up her arms. She must have been brushing against the box flaps without noticing.

"I must remember to stay away from those boxes,"

she muttered as she scrubbed. "And tomorrow I will wear the oldest garment I have."

Thomas held her coat. "Would you like to stop by the hotel for supper?" he offered.

"I won't be fit to eat until I've bathed," she said and shrugged into her coat. "I feel absolutely filthy."

She did take a bath as soon as she arrived home. By then she was unusually hungry.

I should have thought ahead and had something at least partly prepared, she told herself. *I might have known I would be exhausted when I got home.*

Since she didn't feel up to getting a whole meal, she made herself a sandwich. As she ate it, she wished Thomas's offer of supper was still available.

I don't know how Miss Phillips managed to live on snacks, she said to herself. *I would tire of it very quickly.*

As she thought of Miss Phillips, she remembered her recent visit to see the elderly woman. She was still in the local hospital, but Parker had started proceedings to send her to a sanatorium. Berta had objected.

"We can't keep her here," Parker had told her. "We just don't have the facilities."

"Give her a bit more time," Berta had argued. "She should be fine again in a few days."

But Parker had shaken his head. "I'm afraid she will never be fine again, Berta. She's had a dreadful shock— and she wasn't in good condition. She was already so drained of all reserve that she just couldn't cope with it. What do you know about her? She looks like she hasn't eaten properly for months."

Berta then reported to Parker the little that she knew about the older woman. She felt guilty. Surely she should have paid more attention to her. Someone should have intervened, and Berta seemed like the logical person. She had worked with the woman every day.

As she took a sip of her hot tea, Berta wondered if the arrangements for the woman's future had already been made. *She didn't even seem to know me,* she continued her thinking. *Well—at least she won't need to sort through all those—pitiful books.*

Berta was sure that seeing her book-treasures in such an awful state would only have worsened Miss Phillips' condition.

A light rap sounded on her door, then it promptly opened and Glenna stuck her head in. "It's just me," she called.

"Come in," invited Berta, too tired even to get up from her chair.

Glenna came in and deposited a carefully bundled package on the table. "I brought you some pound cake," she said. "Thought you might not feel like baking for the next few days. Thomas said you started in on the library books today."

Berta nodded.

"Was it awful?" asked Glenna.

"Get yourself a cup of tea," Berta invited, and as Glenna went to the cupboard for a cup, she continued. "Yes—it was awful."

"Can you save many?"

"Not many," answered Berta with a shake of her head.

"That's too bad." Glenna poured herself a cup of the tea and took a chair at the table with Berta.

"Is that all you're eating for supper?"

"I didn't feel like cooking."

"Parker says that Miss Phillips must not have cooked for herself for—just ages. He said she was skin and bones."

Berta nodded. "Has Parker decided when—?"

For some reason Berta could not finish the question,

but Glenna knew exactly what she was asking.

"She has already been sent," she answered, then followed with, "The poor old soul. I feel so sorry that no one knew what—state she was in."

They sat in silence.

"I knew—sort of," Berta finally admitted. "Oh, I didn't know for sure—I just suspected. But I should have done something about it."

"What could you have done?"

"I don't know. But there must have been something. What an awful way to live."

Glenna nodded. "You heard about it?"

Berta looked up from her teacup.

"Her place? You heard how she lived?" went on Glenna.

"No," said Berta.

"Parker was over there. She had just one little room. Hardly any heat. No way to cook. She had a box that held a few dishes and her food supplies tucked under her bed—but it was almost empty. Her bed didn't have but one thin blanket and a worn blue pillow and—"

"Stop," said Berta raising her hand. "Please—I don't think I can stand any more."

Glenna took another sip of her tea. "Should I cut some of the pound cake?" she asked brightly. Berta knew it was her effort at diverting attention to something cheerier.

"Please," replied Berta. "I could use some pound cake about now."

Glenna crossed to the cupboard and got a knife from the drawer.

"I was out to see Mama yesterday," she said as she sliced off two thick pieces and placed them on a small plate.

"How is she?"

"About the same. But she keeps cheery enough. She

is knitting mittens for the girls. Guess it helps the hours to pass by."

"I wish she'd move in with me," murmured Berta.

"I think she likes the farm," said Glenna as she carried the cake to the table.

"At least she feeds herself," Berta said as she reached for a piece of the cake.

They ate their cake in silence for a few minutes. Then Berta spoke, her thoughts unwillingly going back to Miss Phillips.

"I still can't understand it," she said. "I mean, she got a salary every month. It should have paid for a decent room and purchased food. Why—"

"She had it all stuffed in her mattress," said Glenna. "They found several hundred dollars."

Berta's mouth dropped open. She could only stare at her younger sister.

———————

Day after miserable day Berta sorted through the boxes of damaged books.

I'm not sure if it's worth the hours, she would tell herself. *There is so little that is still usable.* Still, she stayed at her sorting and filing. The winter weeks passed by one by one. She could hardly wait till it was finally over.

The repair work on the building was in progress. Berta received a weekly report from the mayor. They hoped to have the building habitable by Easter.

"Then we will move the books back in, and you'll be able to get them back on the shelves," he said with satisfaction.

"I'm afraid that will not be a big job, sir," Berta said with a sigh. "I am not finding many that are salvageable."

"I didn't think the fire damage was that extensive," the man said with a frown.

"Not the fire damage, sir. The water damage. That's our biggest problem."

The man looked very disappointed. He began to pace the room, his hands clasped behind his back.

At last he turned back to Berta.

"Well," he said. "We built up a library before—I guess we'll just have to start over and build one again."

Berta nodded.

"You can suit yourself as to how best to go about it," the man continued.

"Me?" asked Berta with surprise.

"Fund-raisers. Campaigns. Bake sales. I don't know how they do these things. I can't remember what was done before. But you'll figure it out."

"But, I—"

"We will give you all the help we can from the town office," the man went on, and he started up his pacing again.

Berta nodded.

"I'm sure the ladies' groups in the city will give their full support. And the schools. The schools helped before."

Berta didn't stir or comment.

"Anyway," the man said and turned to face her, "I'll just leave it entirely up to you. You can go about it any way that you like."

Berta swallowed and nodded her head.

"I'll do what I can," she promised and rose to go.

The library building was ready by Easter. The few boxes of books that were still fit for the shelves were carried back into the building. She spent a few days getting them back in proper order on the new shelves and the file cards set up in the drawer on the check-out table.

Then she straightened to her full height, lifted her

chin, and said with determination, "Well, I guess there's a job to do if we are to fill these shelves again."

She took a deep breath.

"And I guess I'm the only one to do it."

The weeks that followed seemed to blur into each other. When spring came, Berta often longed to be out walking along the swollen waters of the little creek watching the new life return to its banks. But there wasn't time for walking. There was scarcely time for sleeping. Day after day Berta continued her tireless crusade to fill the library shelves.

She used every conceivable means to raise money. She called on every club and congregation in the little town to organize their resources and plan activities that might possibly generate income. Little by little, money came in. As soon as Berta was able to count out a small pile of bills, she sent out book orders. Slowly, ever so slowly, the library shelves were being filled up again with the brightly covered new books.

Berta also accepted donations of secondhand books. As they were obtained, she sorted and cataloged them before placing them on the shelves.

Summer was almost over before the library looked reasonably full once again. It had been a long, slow process involving more time and energy than Berta would have guessed she had.

Though there were still some empty shelves, Berta spoke to Mayor Henderson, suggesting that the library could now be reopened for use.

The man was ecstatic.

"Wonderful," he exclaimed, rubbing his hands together in anticipation. "We'll have a Grand Opening."

He crossed to his desk and studied a sheet that Berta saw was some sort of calendar.

"Let's see—Friday the twenty-fourth looks clear. Yes—that would work just fine."

He looked up at Berta and beamed.

"You go ahead and make whatever plans you think best," he informed her. "Let's make it a real event. Show the folks how much we appreciate our library. Their library. They've worked hard to rebuild. Now we want to show them we appreciate their hard work."

Berta swallowed. She was nearly done in from all the long weeks of hard work. And now this.

Besides, she thought wearily as she rose from the chair and gathered her gloves, *this is election year. A big celebration won't hurt you much, either, will it, Mayor?*

So Berta planned and pushed and organized and labored, and the town library had a Grand Opening. Everyone called it a great success, and the town mayor was able to make a lengthy speech to the citizenry without calling it a re-election bid.

Berta was near exhaustion.

———

"I think I'd like some time off," Berta said to Mayor Henderson just as the neighborhood reapers moved into the harvest fields.

He nodded in agreement.

"You've done a great job," he complimented her. "Folks are saying the new library is even better than the old."

Berta nodded but felt like dropping with weariness.

"Will Miss Saunders be able to look out for things while you're gone?" asked Mayor Henderson.

"I think so," replied Berta, pleased with the young

girl's quickness in learning the library procedures.

"Then you just go ahead and catch yourself a breath," the mayor said jovially. "Take off the whole week if you've a mind to."

Berta looked at the man. A whole week. Did he think he was being generous? Berta was sure she could use a month to get herself rested. She nodded her head. "I think I'll do that, sir," she replied evenly. "The whole week."

Berta walked back to the library to make her plans with Miss Saunders. The girl seemed excited at the idea of being in charge.

Just as Berta left the building she turned back and glanced over the entire room. It did look nice. Though she was nearly worn out, she had a real sense of accomplishment.

She turned back to the young woman behind the desk. "Don't forget to lock the door," she heard herself saying.

Chapter Twenty-one

Illness

For the first two days of her well-earned vacation Berta did nothing but rest and take walks along the creek paths. On the third day she decided she felt rested enough to visit her mother. Thomas was not free to take her in his car, but Berta did not regret that. She decided to walk over to the livery and have the mare hitched up for the trip out of town. It had been some time since she had taken the mare and buggy out.

She was looking forward to a drive in the quiet countryside. It would be as good as a nap in restoring her.

"She needs a run," commented the stable hand as he hitched the horse. "It's been a long time. We do see she gets exercise in the pasture, but that's not the same as going for a drive."

Berta nodded and picked up the reins. She clucked to the mare and they were off.

Berta breathed deeply of the clear fall air and noticed each clump of fall flowers and each bird on the wing.

Autumn, she said to herself. *My favorite time of year.*

Her mind went back to the spontaneous picnic that she and Thomas had shared the year before. It had been pleasant. They'd had little time to enjoy each other's company the past months while Berta had been so busy with the library.

Well—maybe things will settle to a more normal pace now, she thought to herself and hastened the mare on down the road. She was looking forward to the day with her mother.

When she greeted her mother, the woman looked about the same as when Berta had last seen her. She was still busy with knitting and crocheting. But little half-finished projects were scattered from chair to chair or table to table. Berta thought that it seemed a bit strange. Her mother had always been one to finish up one project before starting another.

I guess it has something to do with age, mused Berta, moving a partly knitted sock onto a nearby table so she might sit in the chair.

"How've you been, Mama?" she asked.

"Fine. Just fine," the woman replied.

"I notice you have several things in the works," continued Berta.

Mrs. Berdette chuckled softly. "I guess I must get bored staying with one thing too long," she said.

Berta nodded. "So what are you making here?" she asked, lifting the handwork she had just moved.

Mrs. Berdette frowned. "Let me see it," she asked and accepted the piece of unfinished knitting.

"I don't know what this is," she puzzled, then went on, "It's not mine. It must belong to someone else."

"But you're the only one here," Berta reminded her.

The woman looked more puzzled. "That's right," she said at last. "I live alone now."

Berta was troubled by the conversation, but she did not press her mother further.

"How's your young man?" her mother asked.

"Who?" asked Berta in surprise.

"Your young man? What's his name again? That fellow with the car?"

"You mean Thomas?"

"Thomas. That's right. His name slipped my mind for a minute there."

"Mama—he is not my young man," said Berta firmly.

Her mother looked up quickly from the potholder she was working on.

"He's not? What happened?"

"Nothing happened. He is—he has never been my young man. He is just a friend."

"That's too bad," said her mother shaking her head. "He seemed like such a fine young man."

"And he's not young," Berta added. "We're both past thirty."

Mrs. Berdette looked surprised. "You? Thirty? My—where has the time gone?" She sighed deeply.

"I know," said Berta dryly, "it seems only yesterday."

"What seems like yesterday, dear?" asked Mrs. Berdette.

"Nothing," replied Berta. "I just thought you were going to give your little speech."

Mrs. Berdette smiled. "You and your older sister—"

"I'm the older sister," Berta corrected her. "Remember. I'm Berta. Three years older than Glenna. Remember?"

Mrs. Berdette stopped her needles. She seemed to be puzzling over something. At last she spoke. "You're the oldest. That's right. You're Berta. The younger one is Glenna. That's right."

Berta made no further comment, but her mother's strange words and actions troubled her. She would speak to Parker about it as soon as possible.

———

"Have you been to see Mama lately?" Berta asked Glenna that evening.

"Not since the weekend," said Glenna.

"How did she seem to you?"

"About the same. Why?"

"I was out there today," Berta answered, "and she acted—really confused. Forgetful. I want to speak to Parker about it."

Glenna looked concerned. "He's out on a call right now. I've no idea when he will be home. Do you think we should be worried—about Mama?"

"I don't know. She seemed fine—at times—and then she would say and do strange things."

"Well, she is getting older."

"No." Berta shook her head. "I think it is more than that. She didn't even remember which of us is the older."

Glenna frowned. "That is strange," she said.

"And she has these little work projects scattered all over the house. She couldn't even remember starting one of them."

Glenna looked more worried.

A sound from a bedroom interrupted them. Glenna left her chair and moved quickly toward the door. "The girls both have bad coughs," she explained as she hurried from the room.

Their father is a doctor, for land's sake, thought Berta sourly. *Doesn't he even have time to tend his own children?*

Glenna was soon back again. Berta noticed her slow movement as she lowered herself into a chair.

"You sick?" asked Berta sharply.

"Me? No. Why?"

"You look a bit pale."

"I haven't been feeling too good since—"

"I thought you said you weren't sick," cut in Berta.

"I'm not—sick," replied Glenna.

They sat and looked at each other. "You're pregnant again!" exclaimed Berta.

Glenna nodded.

"My word! Why do you keep having Parker's babies when he never stays home long enough to help you look after them? You're going to wear yourself out."

Glenna said nothing, but Berta saw the hurt in her eyes.

"Berta," said Glenna softly. "What's really bothering you? You've been agitated ever since you walked into the house."

"I'm not—" began Berta, and then she stopped. It was true. She was ready to jump on anyone. She rose from her chair and crossed over to the fire. But she did not apologize to Glenna. She did not know how to apologize to her younger sister.

She stood staring down at the flames and at last turned to face Glenna.

"Mama worries me," she stated flatly. "I had thought Parker would be here. I wanted to talk with him. I hoped he would drive out to the farm and check things out. I don't even like to think of Mama alone out there when we don't know what's going on. What if she's had a little stroke—or something? What if she does something really foolish? We have no idea what—"

"I will speak to Parker as soon as he comes in," said Glenna.

"Well—if you want my opinion, he's gone far too often," stated Berta. "You look about—"

"Berta, listen to me. Parker has provided me with help for the house and help with the children. Parker is a good husband and a great father—in spite of his extremely busy schedule. Please—please don't say unkind things about him."

"Well, you need all the help you can get. You are on every committee and fund-raiser in the city. 'Mrs. Parker Oliver chairs this, organizes that.' It's no wonder you look wan. You're always on the front pages for something—always on the run."

Glenna sighed. "It *is* too much—and sometimes—often—I do tire of it," she admitted. "I know that the—hospital—the city—expects me to—represent many causes. I do get tired of it. But—that's what life is about. Doing what you can—for others."

"Pawsh!" exclaimed Berta. "I think you like to see your own pretty face in print."

It had been years since Berta had spoken so cruelly to Glenna. Both women stared at each other, surprised at the outburst.

"I need to get home," said Berta, gathering her gloves. "I've had a hard day. A hard year, to be exact. I'm exhausted."

Glenna's expression acknowledged Berta's offhanded apology. "I'll tell Parker about Mama as soon as he comes in," she promised quietly.

A child coughed from the bedroom again, and Glenna turned to attend to her. "We'll check on Mama just as soon as we can," she called back over her shoulder.

Berta let herself out. She felt weary. Dejected. Defeated. She had thought she had grown. She had hoped that she had learned many truths from Pastor Talbot's sermons over the months. And now, given a bit of pressure, she had discovered that her old self was lurking just below the surface. She hadn't really changed. She was still simply a product of her past, of her circumstances.

When Parker drove out to the farm that night and checked on Mrs. Berdette, she had already retired for the night. Parker told Berta the next morning that he'd had a hard time explaining to his mother-in-law why he was calling on her at such a late hour.

"She is muddled," he admitted. "I'm not sure at this point just why—but she is confused."

"What can we do?" asked Berta. "She shouldn't be left alone, should she?"

"It would be better if she had someone with her," Parker agreed.

"She is so—set," Berta said. "I've tried and tried to get her to move in with me."

"On the other hand," went on Parker, "a move to new surroundings might only confuse her more. At least she knows her whereabouts at present."

Berta's agitation pressed in upon her. She decided to hitch the mare and head for the farm again.

"Some week of relaxation this is turning out to be," she grumbled to herself as she pressed the mare to quicken her pace.

Mrs. Berdette was watering the garden flowers when Berta arrived. Frost had already stolen their blooms, and they obviously were withered and lifeless. Berta felt despair as she observed her mother's actions.

"What are you doing, Mama?" she couldn't help but ask.

"They must be dry," her mother responded. "They're brown. See?"

"Mama, the frost has already killed them. They're gone for this year," argued Berta and attempted to move her mother back into the house.

"Wait," said the woman. "I didn't get that one yet."

"It's okay, Mama. I'll care for them later," Berta assured her and insisted that her mother return to the kitchen.

Once they were back in the house, her mother brightened. She seemed almost normal for the rest of the morning. Berta began to feel some relief.

"I hear Parker got you out of bed last night," Berta observed.

"Who?"

"Parker."

Mrs. Berdette frowned.

"Glenna's Parker."

"Oh yes. Parker. My, he was out late last night. Was he lost?"

"No, Mama. He just wanted to be sure that you were all right."

Mrs. Berdette smiled. "Isn't that sweet," she said. "Just like Glenna. She must have told him to stop by."

"Mama," said Berta. "I want you to come into town with me."

"A visit would be nice," said Mrs. Berdette. "I'll get my hat. Is it chilly enough for a shawl?"

"Not for a visit, Mama. I want you to come and live with me."

The woman stopped midstride. "Oh, I couldn't do that, dear," she said quickly. "Someone has to take care of the team."

"Mama, we don't have a team anymore," argued Berta.

The woman looked confused. "We don't? What happened to them?"

Berta gave up. It was clear that her mother could not be left alone.

"Mama, I'm going to go pack some things for you, and then I'm taking you home with me," she announced. She was going to accept no excuses.

"That's nice, dear," said Mrs. Berdette. "You were always my helper. I always depended on you. For everything. 'Berta is my dependable one,' I used to say."

Berta stopped in her tracks. "Then why did you always favor Glenna?" she asked sharply.

"Glenna," said her mother. "Oh my. I didn't favor Glenna."

"You did," argued Berta. "You always treated us—differently."

"Of course," said her mother in agreement. "I had to. You were different."

"But—"

"What would you have had me do? Put Glenna in straight skirts? Crop off her hair? Or insist that you wear ribbons and bows? You both were different. It wouldn't have been fair to make either one of you a copy of the other. Would it?"

Berta had nothing more to say. She went to pack a suitcase.

———

It had seemed like a good idea to take her mother into town, but it turned out to be far more difficult to manage than Berta had anticipated.

She had to go back to work. Her mother could not be left alone while she was off for the day at the library. She could not take her mother with her to the library. Nor was she successful in finding someone to stay with her mother at the house. In the end, Glenna took their mother in to be with her family. Berta knew it was a hardship for the busy Glenna. But there seemed little she could do about it.

"I'll pop in to give a hand when I can," she promised.

But after a day at the library, there seemed so little time left to help out at Glenna's.

Berta felt her life was whirling out of control. She also felt that she had lost all of the spiritual ground she had gained over the previous months. It troubled her deeply.

"I am who I am," she said wearily one evening as she prepared for bed, trying to find an acceptable excuse, but in her heart she knew she felt defeated by another hard day.

Her spoken words did little to make her feel any better.

Chapter Twenty-two

The Sermonette

"Mama's much better." Glenna announced the good news to Berta as they stood on the steps of the church watching little Rosie and their mother hand in hand, chatting with the minister.

"Her mind seems much clearer. Parker says it may have been a little stroke. But I don't suppose we'll ever know for sure. Sometimes these things happen."

Berta looked again toward their mother. She did seem better. It was a great relief.

"Perhaps I can take her with—"

"Not yet," Glenna interrupted. "Parker says she shouldn't be moved—shouldn't face another change just yet. We don't want a setback."

Berta was a bit annoyed. Were they thinking that living with her would cause her mother to relapse? Was her company really that intolerable?

"In a week or so—perhaps," Glenna explained. "Parker thinks the children are good for her right now. They seem to brighten her up. She does enjoy them so."

Berta nodded. She certainly couldn't offer her mother children. Clearly Glenna was taking care of that.

She knew her sister's next baby was due in a few days. "What will Mama do while you're—indisposed?" she asked, seeking to keep the rancor out of her voice.

"Mrs. Rudi will be living in. Mama will be just fine." Berta nodded.

Better to have her with an unknown housekeeper than her own daughter? she felt like commenting, but she bit her tongue.

"I'm glad she's getting better," Berta said instead and turned to go.

———

Glenna's new baby was a boy. Berta thought it likely that everyone would compare him to Jamie. But there was really little likeness. At least in appearance. For some reason unknown to her, Berta was relieved. It would have been so hard to look at a little reminder of Jamie day after day.

Mrs. Berdette seemed to take on a new glow as she fussed over the little one.

"I think having a baby to care for is good for Mama," Glenna said.

I hope you don't plan on keeping her supplied, Berta thought dourly.

Glenna had already produced four babies. In Berta's thinking, that was quite enough.

"She loves to sit and rock him—and sing to him. It's the first I've heard some of those little songs since I was a child. It's so sweet," Glenna commented.

Berta nodded. *You had more songs than I did,* she wished to tell Glenna. *Mama never cuddled me like she did you.*

But Berta turned away.

———

"Where's Mama?" Berta asked as she hung her coat in the hall closet at Glenna's house and moved toward the kitchen.

"She's rocking Tyrone."

"Where are the girls?" asked Berta.

"Rosie is reading to Anna. Parker brought them some new books."

"And Parker?" asked Berta tersely.

"He'll be home soon. He's making a check at the hospital. He had an appendectomy last night."

"He had an appendectomy? My—he's doing well—to be home so soon."

Glenna just smiled at Berta's bit of sarcasm.

"You know what I mean," she said and led the way to the kitchen.

"Sounds like we're all accounted for," said Berta dryly.

"Well—not quite all," replied Glenna as she busied herself with Christmas cooking at the big range with its enameled front. Berta had never seen such a fancy stove.

"Thomas is coming," said Glenna matter-of-factly.

Berta stopped dishing out the pickles.

"I thought Christmas was a family affair," she said.

"It is. Family and guests. Occasionally I like to include a guest. Folks who don't have family near. Pastor has been preaching on opening your door of hospitality."

Berta had shut off that sermon, arguing that a single woman could not easily follow through on it anyway.

"And Parker says . . ." continued Glenna.

If I hear "Parker says" one more time, I think I'll scream, thought Berta.

" . . . that we don't really have folks in our home often enough. He says I can get all the help I need—and he'll do his best to be here. He misses male companionship. He enjoys Thomas."

So it seemed to be settled. Berta turned back to the pickles. At least Glenna had not said she felt Thomas would make the perfect mate for Berta. For that Berta was thankful—but she still wondered if that wasn't the plan.

———

"Mama would like to go out to the farm and pick up a few more things," Glenna told Berta the next Sunday. "Parker is not free to go—and I hate to take little Tyrone out. Would you be free to help Mama?"

Berta nodded assent.

"Parker says the road right now is not to be trusted for an auto, but you are more than welcome to use his team and sleigh. Do you think Thomas would mind driving?"

"Why don't you ask him?" retorted Berta.

Glenna smiled sweetly. "I'll do that," she said, seeming to take no offense.

It was a sunny, mild day in spite of the fact that the snow lay deep across the fields. Berta checked her mother to make sure that she was well bundled under the lap robes.

Parker's team was spirited. Berta was glad she wasn't doing the driving. Thomas held the reins with confidence and seemed to enjoy handling the team.

"This is nice," Mrs. Berdette commented, looking about. "I miss the country."

Berta soon realized what Parker meant by the road not being in any condition for a car. There were drifts of snow across the entire road in places, but they posed no problem to the team.

"I miss looking out at the fields," mused Mrs. Berdette. "It isn't the same to look at buildings. You can't really see—anything."

Berta could not help but be amused. Glenna's home was in the best part of the city—with wide lawns and beautiful houses. What would her mother think if she was on one of the streets where the houses crowded in closely to one another?

The outing in the sharp country air seemed to loosen Mrs. Berdette's tongue. She continued little discourses and comments the whole way. For the most part Berta just listened. Thomas and her mother seemed to be having a good chat about the neighbors who used to live at the various farms. Berta wondered how many of them were still inhabited by the original family members— and how many had been sold off to strangers.

"Glenna's little ones are so sweet," Mrs. Berdette suddenly interjected into the current topic.

Thomas nodded with a smile.

"You know, children can be so different," went on Mrs. Berdette. "They each have their own personality from the day they are born."

Thomas looked interested but said nothing.

"Rosie is such a little—mother. She busies herself looking after the two little ones. She fusses over little animals in the same way. Always taking care of things. Anna, now—she enjoys the fussing. She wants Rosie to wait on her hand and foot. Oh yes, she takes full advantage of Rosie's willingness to do so."

She chuckled, and Thomas joined her.

"Little Jamie was independent and outgoing right from the start. He picked his special people. Yes, he did. He favored certain folk—even certain family members. Little Tyrone now—he loves everyone—just like Glenna. I think he'll be much like his mother. So warm and affectionate. A cuddler. I love to hold a cuddler. He just snuggles right down against you and seems to almost purr. Glenna was like that."

Mrs. Berdette stopped and chuckled again.

"Not Berta," she laughed. "Oh no, not Berta. Why, from the time she was newborn I couldn't get her to cuddle. She wanted her independence. She'd rear back and push away from me and look around with those big eyes, just as though she was sizing up the world to determine exactly what she wanted from it. That was Berta."

She laughed affectionately.

Berta stirred in her seat. Her mother's comments were making her uncomfortable. She wondered if Thomas was feeling uncomfortable as well. He looked completely at ease. Berta wondered if she should speak or cough to remind her mother that she was still in the second seat of the sleigh.

"Well—I've always felt that you had to let a child be who he is. Oh, you try to shape him to be the best person he can be—and you pray—that God will help with the shaping. But you can't force a child to be—like someone else. You can't. And you can't compare him to someone else, either. It's like oranges and apples. You have to measure and love each child for who he is."

Thomas nodded. "Sounds wise to me," he responded.

"Take our two girls," Mrs. Berdette continued, and Berta squirmed again. She was not enjoying her mother's chatter.

"They were different from day one. And the same traits that I saw in them as infants, I still see now. Berta's always been strong and independent. Capable. My—how many times I've leaned on Berta."

Stop it, Berta wanted to say. *Stop it, Mama. This whole rambling conversation is an embarrassment.*

"I needed Berta—so many times over the years—and

I've thanked God for her so often. A no-nonsense child. A no-nonsense woman. She always was able—"

She stopped. Berta fervently hoped she would not go on.

"Now, Glenna," said her mother and her voice took on sparkle. "Glenna was my sunshine. She made life better by just being there. Everyone loved Glenna."

"She must have been a beautiful child," commented Thomas.

"Oh—she was. No one could deny that. But it was more than her—cuteness. You know, I've seen some pretty children that one couldn't stand to even be around. No—it wasn't the prettiness. It was the—attitude. Yes, attitude. Even a child can have an attitude." She paused a moment, then said, "I've never really thought of it that way before—but, of course, they have an attitude. That's what makes us all different, don't you think? Our attitude."

"I guess that's a good part of it, all right," agreed Thomas.

"Yes," mused Mrs. Berdette. "That's it. Two people could look just alike—yet be different. I knew a set of twins once—couldn't have looked more alike. One was bright and cheery—the other sullen and—and cross all the time. Then she couldn't figure out why the other twin had all the friends."

Mrs. Berdette chuckled again.

"As a child, I wondered about it, too," she went on. "Now I know."

"Attitude," said Thomas.

"You know," said Mrs. Berdette, her voice and expression alive with excitement that she had hit on one of the secrets of life. "I'll wager—no, I wouldn't wager— what does one say in place of that word? Anyway, I'm sure—quite sure—that it really doesn't matter that much what one has—or even how one looks—it's attitude that determines what your life will be."

Thomas nodded.

"How one sees God," said Mrs. Berdette softly. It was as though she had forgotten both Thomas and Berta and was working things through for herself. "How one sees God—that's so important. We have to see things as God sees them. We have to learn how to—to agree with Him—on everything."

She paused, then said, "And how one thinks of others. We have to see others as God sees them. That's it. If you get that all straightened out—then you'll have the right attitude about yourself. That's it."

She turned to Thomas. "You know," she said, "I think that's a much easier lesson for some people than for others."

Thomas nodded again. Berta was thankful they were turning in at the farm gate.

————

It didn't take long for Berta to help her mother gather up the things she had come to collect. The unused house was cold, and they were all anxious to get back to town. A slight wind had come up and the day was getting more blustery.

"Oh yes," said Mrs. Berdette as they were about to leave. "I need my medicine."

"What medicine?" asked Berta. "I didn't know you were taking medicine."

"Oh—not real medicine. Just herbs," said her mother and went off to the medicine chest to pick up what she wanted.

Berta tucked the bottles in the bag with the knitting

materials and hurried her mother out the door to the waiting sleigh.

Much to Berta's relief, the trip back to town was a quieter one.

Chapter Twenty-three

Gaining Ground

In spite of her determination to push the thoughts from her mind, Berta could not help but ponder her mother's comments to Thomas on their trip to the farm. In the days that followed, questions kept coming to the surface of her mind. Was it really attitude? Or was it circumstances that shaped a life? She had always felt her attitude had been formed by the fact that she had been born plain, while her baby sister had been born beautiful. Wasn't that the issue? Wasn't that why she'd had to fight her way through life? People just gravitated to attractive things. And to attractive persons. People shunned her. Well, no. They didn't shun her, but they certainly didn't make over her like they had over her baby sister.

Dependable. That's what her mother had said of her. Well, she'd really had no choice. That's all there was left for her to be. She couldn't change her plain looks. She couldn't become sparkly and bright like Glenna.

Wasn't that part of what her mother had said? You were who you were. Even parents couldn't change that.

Yes—she was Berta. Shaped by her circumstance.

Or was it by her attitude toward her circumstance? She couldn't seem to sort it out.

"Do you think our past shapes us?" she asked Thomas as they walked home from the morning service together.

"Shapes us?"

"Influences who we become?"

There was silence while Thomas worked through his answer.

"Yes—of course—but not totally," he responded at last.

"What do you mean?" He didn't sound any more conclusive than she had been. Berta had wanted some solid answers.

"Well—we aren't at the mercy of our circumstances," he replied firmly.

Berta turned to study his face. There were still questions in her eyes.

"We still have choices," he went on. "We still have the will—the choice—to determine what we wish to accept or reject. What we make of the experience."

"Even as a child?" Her words were too sharp.

He looked at her evenly, seeming to try to read her thoughts, to think carefully before he answered.

"As a child we might be unduly influenced. We might misunderstand—misinterpret. We haven't built much of a base for understanding relationships—life. We might even make wrong judgments that certainly have long-range effects but—but one day we need to come to the place where we rethink things. Where we carefully weigh things and—and take responsibility for who we are. We can't keep looking back. Laying all the credit—or blame—for what we have become on what we have experienced."

"You think children can misinterpret?"

"I know they can."

He fell silent. Berta wondered what he was thinking.

"When I was a child," he began, "I wanted a bike. In the worst way. I longed for a bike. I dreamed of a bike. I even prayed for a bike. Then Buddy Albert's dad bought him a bike. It was exactly like my dream-bike. Buddy did a lot of bragging. A lot of showing off. He taunted me with the fact that his folks loved him so much that they'd do anything for him.

"So, I got the notion that I didn't get a bike because my pa didn't love me."

He stopped. He seemed intent on carefully watching each place that he put his foot for his next step.

"I made such a big thing of it in my own mind that I was totally convinced I was unloved. I watched for things—little things—to support my supposition. And I found them, too. Lots of them. Soon I had built a real case against my pa."

He stopped again.

"I likely would have gone all through life convinced I wasn't loved if—if there hadn't been another little incident."

He chuckled softly. Berta raised her head to see why the sudden humor.

"I was sent out to get the cows. We had this old red bull. He was usually dependable, but this one night I was feeling mad about something—likely sore that I wasn't loved—I mean, having to do farm chores was proof of that, wasn't it?"

He chuckled again.

"Anyway, I was having a mad, so I sicced the dog on that old bull. He didn't take too kindly to that, and he turned and came after the dog. Of course, the dog tucked his tail between his legs and ran for cover—which was me. The bull didn't even hesitate. He came for me, too. I was so scared I just froze right to the spot. I could see that red bull coming right for me, his head down, nostrils flaring, and I knew I was going to die. I just knew it.

"I never will know where he came from, but suddenly I felt myself being hoisted out of the way. Pa was there. He lifted me out of the path of the bull just in time. He didn't have time to get himself clear. The bull caught him with one horn and sent him flying. He had two broken ribs. But do you know what he said when he scrambled up out of the dust? He said, 'Are you okay, son?' and when I said I was, he said, 'Thank God.' Just 'Thank God' and he put his face in his hands and his shoulders shook.

"He managed to get himself off the ground, and we went back to the house hand in hand. I could never convince myself again that my pa didn't love me."

Berta felt the tears in her throat. She still didn't have things sorted out, but she had much to think about.

"Mama's taken a bad turn." Glenna's expression was grave. She had come into the library and whispered the words to Berta.

Berta felt fear gripping her. She motioned toward the small private room.

"What's happened?" she asked as she pulled Glenna in behind her and closed the door.

"We don't know. She didn't get up this morning, so I went to check on her. She—she looks strange."

"Is she—saying strange things again?"

"She's not saying anything. That's what frightens me," said Glenna. "She—she looks like she's in some kind of—stupor."

"What does Parker say?" Berta never thought that she would be asking that question. She had become so irritated with Glenna's constant reference to Parker's opinion.

"He's baffled. He doesn't think it's a stroke. He can't figure what is wrong. He's with her now."

"I'll come," said Berta, quickly making up her mind. "I just have to tell my assistant."

"I'll wait for you outside," said Glenna. "I've got the auto."

"You're driving?" Berta was shocked.

"Parker says I shouldn't be tied to home just because he can't get away," replied Glenna over her shoulder. "He taught me."

Berta said nothing more but hurried to inform Miss Saunders of her plans. Soon she was joining Glenna in the auto.

"It's so strange," Glenna said as they drove through the streets. "She was just fine when she went to bed last night."

Then Glenna corrected herself. "No—that's not quite right. I've noticed that she has been a bit hazy the last few days. Sometimes she is perfectly clear and then—"

"Well, she was perfectly clear when we drove out to the farm last Sunday afternoon. I've never heard Mama so full of chatter."

"It's strange," Glenna mused. "Very strange."

———————

"I think I've solved our mystery."

Parker met them in the hallway as soon as they got to the house.

"How's Mama?" asked Berta quickly.

Parker turned to her. In his hand he carried some bottles. Berta recognized them as the ones she had helped her mother place in her bag with the knitting.

"Mama's medicine," she exclaimed, pointing to the bottles in Parker's hand.

"Medicine?" said Glenna. "I didn't know Mama was on medicine."

"It's not medicine really—just some silly herbs," said Berta. "How is she?"

"She's sleeping," replied Parker.

"Is she—?" began Glenna.

"She's much better now. I pumped her stomach."

Both women looked at Parker in surprise.

"I got suspicious when I found these bottles on her dresser. Then Rosie said that Gramma took 'a whole bunch' because she said she hadn't had any for a long time, so I decided to pump her stomach. She had taken 'a whole bunch' all right."

"But they're just harmless herbs," maintained Berta.

"Yes—they likely are—I'm not sure of that yet, not having had a chance to get them analyzed," admitted Parker. "Taken properly and separately, they are likely quite harmless—perhaps some of them are even beneficial. But taken as Mama did, they were almost deadly."

"Deadly?" Glenna looked pale. Parker reached out an arm to support her.

"It could have been very serious, my dear," he admitted. "But she seems to be rallying now. Oh, she may still be confused until it is out of her system, but I think she'll be fine."

"Is that what happened before?" asked Berta.

"I'm sure it is," replied the doctor. "She has likely been taking these in the wrong combination for months—thinking that she was doing herself good."

"Oh, dear!" exclaimed Glenna. "What if we hadn't discovered . . ."

Parker's arm tightened. "I've just put on the kettle for a fresh pot of tea," he said. "Why don't you go have a cup?

I think we could all use one."

"I want to look in on Mama first," said Glenna, and she moved toward the bedroom, Berta close at her heels.

Mrs. Berdette seemed to be sleeping peacefully. The color was back in her face, and her breathing was soft and even.

"I think she'll be fine," Parker repeated as assurance. Both women relaxed and allowed themselves to be led to the kitchen. Mrs. Rudi was there, putting a roast in the oven for supper.

Glenna gathered tea things on a tray and led the way to the living room. Parker was already putting on his heavy coat.

"Aren't you staying?" asked Glenna. "I thought you said you needed a cup."

"I gulped one quickly in the kitchen," he replied as he kissed Glenna on the cheek. "I need to get back to the hospital. Have someone come for me if you need me—but I think things will be fine now."

She nodded.

"He is so busy," Glenna said to Berta as the door closed on Parker.

"I don't know how you stand it," Berta said with candid criticism. "I think if I had a husband, I'd want him home—at least occasionally."

"Berta," spoke Glenna in a scolding tone, "don't carry on so. Parker is a wonderful husband, and well you know it."

Berta was surprised at Glenna's words, but especially of her manner. The only time Glenna ever spoke with such frank intensity was when she was defending Parker.

Berta took her tea and pulled her chair closer to the fire. She felt exhausted. They'd had another scare. Thankfully, it seemed that they had avoided a crisis and made an important discovery. And that, too, was due to Doctor Parker.

"I feel drained," said Glenna. "I was so worried."

Berta nodded. "Well—at least we agree on that," she replied simply.

To her surprise Glenna chuckled—perhaps a nervous reaction. Berta looked at her quickly. Was she reacting— giddily?

But Glenna looked perfectly in control.

"Oh, Berta," she said, and she leaned back in her chair and reached her hand out to the warmth of the fire. "There has not been much that we have agreed about over the years, has there?"

Berta felt confused and a bit alarmed. She did not remember ever having a candid discussion over personal things like this with Glenna.

"I guess there hasn't been," Berta finally agreed.

"Except for Parker," said Glenna.

"Parker?"

"We both loved Parker—remember?"

Berta felt her cheeks flush. "That's a—a rather strong word and—that was a long time ago," she hurried to inform Glenna. "I certainly don't—"

"I know," said Glenna. "I sometimes wonder if you even like him now."

"Of course I do," argued Berta sitting bolt upright. "It's just—just that he seems so—so important."

Glenna sat up too.

"You don't care much for important people, do you?"

"What do you mean?"

Glenna shrugged. "I don't know. I just—just feel you—bristle when—when someone gets—attention. Why?"

"I—I don't think I—bristle," retorted Berta.

"Yes—you do. I've felt it—often."

Berta was silent. But she could not evade Glenna's direct question. Did she bristle? Did she resent important people? Did it bother her when someone got special attention?

Maybe. Maybe it did. Maybe it went back to when they were children.

"Maybe it's because when we were little, you got all the attention," she dared to say.

"But I didn't," replied Glenna. "I distinctly remember Papa teaching you to ride—to handle the horses—how to plant the corn—and even how to hold a fishing rod. Don't you remember?"

Berta nodded slowly.

"I didn't get to learn any of those things," said Glenna.

Berta said nothing. She had always known there was a special bond between herself and her father.

"And Granna—remember who she taught to knit—to care for her special flowers? She wouldn't let me near them."

"That's because I was older," argued Berta.

"And who learned to bake cookies? Who got to read the storybooks—to the whole family? And they listened—every night—both Mama and Papa. And who had the special school projects that took hours of tramping through the woods and meadows so that you could collect your—what did you call them—specimens?"

"But—"

Glenna waved her to silence.

"And in school. Who did the teachers call on to explain a math problem to the class or to set up the lab equipment for an experiment?"

"Glenna, were you jealous?" asked Berta.

Glenna laughed. A soft, joyous laugh. "Jealous? I was proud. Proud! You were my big sister and I walked in your shadow—but I loved it."

"Then why—? I don't follow—"

"Because I don't think you understand how things really were. I don't think you know—have ever known—how others see you. You seem to—to have this—this image of Berta Berdette that is far less than who you really are—and I don't know where it came from."

Berta stirred restlessly.

"Take another look at yourself, Berta. Others see you as—"

"I don't care what others think," Berta cut in sharply.

To her surprise Glenna laughed again.

Then she sobered. "Oh, Berta," she said, and there was affection in her voice. "That's one of the things I have loved about you. Have even envied. You have never cared what others think. It doesn't bother you a fig. I've spent a—a lifetime—trying to please—everybody. Trying to be pleasant. Sometimes I think it's a load no one should have to carry."

"Then why did you?"

Glenna sobered and shrugged. To Berta's surprise her sister's eyes filled with tears. She put her teacup down and reached for a hankie.

"Because," she said with a shake of her piled-up curls, "because—it would have made so much—so much unhappiness—for others. I couldn't have stood that."

"That's where we're different. It wouldn't have mattered to me."

There was silence.

Berta broke it. "But you surprise me," she said, and her tone had lost its sharp edge.

Glenna just looked at her, still blinking away unwanted tears.

"I always thought that you were just naturally—sugary," said Berta.

"Naturally? Oh no. No, it's not natural. Not even easy. I've been—shamed so many times by—what has gone on inside. Oh, I try so hard to be—sweet and—good—but sometimes I don't feel at all sweet—or good, either. I want to say 'Why me?' or 'That's your problem.' "

Her cheeks flushed.

"It amazes me at times how dreadfully—selfish—I feel inside. I need to—to constantly be praying for God's help to—to say the right thing—do the right thing. Even as a child, I constantly was asking God to help me. I know it's dreadful to be so—so self-seeking—when—when God has given so much—of himself—for me. When there is so much—need all around us. When people hurt and—and I still desire to please myself.

"But God does help me—He really does—when I ask Him, when I take the time to pray."

Berta could only stare. She would never have guessed that her sister had worked so hard, at such personal sacrifice, to be good. To be what she felt her God wanted her to be.

"I never knew," she said slowly. "I just thought—but I admire you for—for—"

Glenna sniffed and blew.

"I just thought," Berta said again awkwardly, "that you were as—as prissy as you were pretty."

Glenna smiled.

"I guess we have never been able to—to tell each other how we really feel."

"No," agreed Berta, shaking her head. "I guess we haven't. We haven't even tried."

"Do you think it's too late?" asked Glenna frankly. "I mean, do you think we could learn to talk? Could be— friends?"

"Well, I—I—" began Berta. "Friends?"

"Forget the past misconceptions?" prompted Glenna.

"Misconceptions?" echoed Berta. "I guess there may have been—sort of—misconceptions."

"I do love you, Berta," said Glenna softly, and her eyes filled with tears again. "I always have."

"And I—I guess . . ."

But Berta could not finish her statement. She crossed to Glenna, who had already risen from her chair and moved toward her, her arms reaching out for her embrace. They wept on each other's shoulder. It was the first time Berta truly allowed herself the comfort of tears.

Chapter Twenty-four

The Decision

"Come in, Miss Berdette," the minister said and pointed the way into his office. "It's a very pleasant day, isn't it? A nice day for a stroll."

Berta nodded agreement and took the chair the pastor indicated. She unbuttoned her coat and pushed it back. Already she felt too warm.

"How is your mother?" he asked with genuine interest.

"She's just fine now," Berta answered.

"So Doctor Oliver's assumption was right. It was the combination of herbs she had been using?"

"Apparently."

"Well, I'm glad the solution was found before real harm could be done," the man said.

Berta nodded.

It wasn't her mother whom she had come to discuss, but she did not know where to start.

"You asked to see me," said the minister. That helped a bit. Berta took a deep breath.

"I've—I've been trying to—to sort through some things," she confessed honestly. "I have come to the conclusion that I need some—guidance."

The minister nodded.

"There have been so many things," said Berta, letting her gaze fall to the clenched hands in her lap.

The minister waited.

"When you first came—first started your—your sermons on God, I was so excited. I knew that I had—that I needed to learn more about Him—who He is and how He—what He wants of me."

Berta was stumbling along. She didn't know if she was even making any sense.

"And then there was that library fire and I got so busy—and I sort of—dropped out. I mean—I stopped reading my Bible. I didn't even pray some days. And pretty soon I—I was right back where I started."

"And where had you started?" the minister asked softly.

Berta bowed her head.

"I'm not sure," she admitted. She looked up at the man across the desk.

She decided to start at the beginning.

"I was the firstborn," she said and seemed to think her words would explain something. The man listened carefully.

"And then Glenna was born."

He nodded again. Berta dropped her eyes.

"Well—I was—Glenna was beautiful—right from the beginning," explained Berta.

"And you weren't?"

"No. No—I was always plain."

"I see."

"Everywhere we went, people all fussed over Glenna."

Berta was silent again.

"You felt—left out?"

"Well—yes—I guess I did. I think that it—angered me that Glenna got all the attention. I think I was hurt."

Silence.

"You can understand that, can't you? I was just a child. I needed to know—I wanted people to notice me, too."

"Of course," said the man.

"It was like that all our growing-up years—Glenna getting fussed over. Me—?" Berta shrugged.

"Did you take it out on Glenna?"

"How do you mean?"

"Were you mean to her? Did you show bitterness?"

"I suppose I did—some. But not much—given the circumstances."

"The circumstances?"

Berta swallowed. Silence again.

"So, how is this troubling you now?" asked the man.

Berta shook her head. "I—I don't know. I can't really explain. It's just that lately—lately I've—I've been talking to people—I've done a great deal of thinking."

"Yes . . ."

"Thomas said that children often misinterpret incidents in their childhood."

"I agree with Thomas."

"And Mama went on and on about how she has always—counted on me. I've been her—dependable one."

"She's told me the same thing," said the pastor. "Many times and in many ways." He smiled.

"But I wanted to be loved—not depended upon," declared Berta.

"And you don't think she loved you?"

Berta shook her head. "Not like Glenna."

"Perhaps we should leave Glenna out of this for the moment," the minister said.

Berta wondered how Glenna could be left out. Wasn't that the whole issue?

"Did your parents ever tell you they loved you?" asked the minister.

"Yes, of course," admitted Berta.

"Did they say they would love you 'if'—or love you 'when'—or love you 'because'?" asked Pastor Talbot.

"No . . . never," she said slowly.

"Then why did you find it so hard to believe them? Why did you think they would lie to you?"

"I'm sure they wouldn't lie," Berta quickly responded.

"But you didn't believe them."

"Well—I—I'm sure that they thought they loved me. I'm sure—"

"But you didn't think they did?"

Berta shifted in her seat. It was terribly warm in the room.

"I—I'm sure they did," she admitted. "I—mean I didn't really feel—unloved."

"Just not loved as much as Glenna?"

It was an embarrassing question.

"Let's go a step further," said the minister. "Because of this—feeling in childhood, how do you feel about yourself now?"

Berta thought about this question. It was very difficult to answer.

"I—I still—still struggle," she admitted.

"Your confidence is threatened?"

"I—I guess so."

He smiled again. "I'm sure most people would be as surprised to hear that as am I. You seem so self-assured."

"It's false," said Berta rather sharply.

"Making us feel inferior—unworthy—is the devil's work," went on the pastor. "He even tried it on Christ himself. 'Prove that you're somebody,' he taunted Christ.

'Make the world take notice of you.' I think in one way or another, he says that to all of us. Along with it comes the subtle message, 'You're a nobody, and you know it.' 'You're really not worth anything.' "

Berta looked surprised.

"But that isn't what God says," continued the man. "God says each of us is special. Created for a special reason—to fulfil a special task. He loved us so much that He sent His Son, Jesus, to die. Now if we are that important, we must be worth a great deal—to Him.

"You are special, Miss Berdette. Not just to your family—but to God himself. Do you believe that? I mean, can you honestly claim the love of God?"

Berta felt herself begin to tremble. Did she really believe that God loved her?

"I—I—need to work on that," she admitted. "It's hard for me—"

"It's hard for any of us—but if we really, really can take in that truth, we are free to be whatever God wants us to be."

"In spite of the circumstances of the past?" asked Berta candidly.

He nodded. "Our past really has less to do with it than we might think," he said, and drew out a sheet of paper and picked up a pencil. As he talked he scribbled notes on the paper and drew little diagrams to emphasize his points.

"You see—we do have reasons to be doubters. First of all—we are born into a world that has been spoiled by sin. It was a good world—God himself called it good, but then sin entered. And sin remains—so sin has ruined the world we live in, and even though we ourselves can be forgiven our sin—sin still affects the world we live in.

"Secondly, we come to the world as children. We have no previous knowledge of our world. Of relationships with others. We gather our information as we go, but we have little knowledge or base on which to build—so, like Thomas said, we often make mistakes in our judgments, in our interpretation of what we gather. And children are so impressionable. Those false assumptions are often magnified.

"Thirdly, Satan always makes the most of all wrong information. He makes sure that it is reinforced, time and again, until he uses it against us, convincing us that we are just what he has told us we are. Useless. Unloved. To blame. Guilty. Whatever it is that he has been trying to impress upon us.

"Now, we can't undo the past—and how we have read the information we've gathered. Maybe we have been right. Maybe we have been wrong. But regardless, we— as adults—must come to a time when we take an honest look at who God says we are and make our own decision based on His."

"One can change?"

"We really are who we decide to be. That is how God has made us. With a free choice. If we were totally the victims of circumstances—God would be dreadfully unfair. But we can choose. Two people—given the same set of circumstances—can choose—one for good, the other to his own destruction. It all comes back to one thing. Our choices. Our attitude."

"Attitude," said Berta. "That's what Mama said."

The pastor nodded.

"And our attitude can show up very early in life," continued the pastor.

Her mama had said that too.

Then to Berta's mind came the words of her mother from many years before: *"Berta, I fear to think what that defiant spirit might cost you."* Berta felt close to tears.

"So it's been me—all along," she said, her voice soft and trembly.

"Understanding ourselves is the first step," said the minister. "And it is a big step. If we understand our motives—our attitude—it gives us opportunity to accept—or to change—how we think or what we do with our lives. All of us have some things that we need to change. Only with God's help can we do that."

The remainder of their time together was spent searching through the pastor's well-marked Bible, studying verses that suddenly came alive for Berta. She began to see herself in a totally different light.

———

Over the days that followed Berta spent much time in prayer and study of her Bible. More and more she was understanding God—but she was also understanding herself.

I have refused to love because I thought myself unlovable, she admitted one night after reading of God's great love for her.

Even little Jamie. Even Jamie. I could not even tell Jamie that I loved him.

Berta lowered her head to her folded arms and wept.

———

Little by little Berta began to change. Rosie and Anna seemed to notice it. They ran eagerly to greet Aunt Berty each Sunday. Berta even dropped by mid-week, just to chat with her nieces or share in a child's tea party. She didn't notice her mother and Glenna exchange tearful glances.

Little Tyrone tottered toward her when she made an

Looking for More Good Books to Read?

You can find out what is new and exciting with previews, descriptions, and reviews by signing up for Bethany House newsletters at

www.bethanynewsletters.com

We will send you updates for as many authors or categories as you desire so you get only the information you really want.

Sign up today!

A New Series Depicting the Challenges and Enduring Faith of the Early Settlers

After graduating in May of 1900, Andrew Bjorklund and Ellie Wold make plans to marry once the harvest is over and their new house is finished in Blessing, North Dakota. They spend the summer working hard, and the Lord seems to shine on them with favor. But when their new barn burns—and many of their possessions and dreams with it—how will they fare in this hard, unforgiving land? Will they be able to keep their faith when the life they looked forward to is now unraveling?